"I DO NOT WISH TO MAKE ANY APOLOGY TO YOU. BUT I AM WILLING TO MAKE AMENDS."

"There is something." His voice, low and intense, alerted her to a change in him. "You could kiss me," he said. "A kiss for every trout your brothers have cost me."

"You can't be serious."

"But I am. Our bargain will be just between us."

She didn't move.

His hands went to her waist, and he nestled her lightly between his legs. "I want one now." His lips touched hers . . .

ϾϾϾϾϾϾϾϾϾϾϾϾϾϾϾϾϾϾϾϾϾϾϾϾϾϾϾϾϾϾ

"As poignant and lovely as a Regency 'A Room With A View' "
Meagan McKinney, author of *Lions and Lace*

"A wonderfully tender, sensual love story . . . Bel Shaw is a captivating heroine."
Anthea Malcolm, author of *Touch of Scandal*

Other Regency Romances from Avon Books

Sweet Bargain

KATE MOORE

AVON BOOKS ◆ NEW YORK

SWEET BARGAIN is an original publication of Avon Books. This work has never before appeared in book form. This work is a novel. Any similarity to actual persons or events is purely coincidental.

AVON BOOKS
A division of
The Hearst Corporation
1350 Avenue of the Americas
New York, New York 10019

Copyright © 1993 by Kate Moore
Published by arrangement with the author
Library of Congress Catalog Card Number: 92–96998
ISBN: 0–380–77056–3

First Avon Books Printing: March 1993

AVON TRADEMARK REG. U.S. PAT. OFF. AND IN OTHER COUNTRIES, MARCA REGISTRADA, HECHO EN U.S.A.

Printed in the U.S.A.

RA 10 9 8 7 6 5 4 3 2 1

In memory of
Linda Bek Drewry
1947–1992

A heroine in her own right

Prologue

&&&&&&&&&&&

Monday morning

Dear Tom,

What an ungrateful little sister I shall prove to be if I don't answer your letter at once. But how am I to invent matter sufficient for a true epistle out of my adventures in Hampshire? You at least have the Turks to furnish an anecdote or two.

Last night another Shaw family dinner. There, I may now put down my pen and consider myself the most thorough correspondent, for I know that the very phrase "family dinner" conjures up at least a hundred closely written lines of detail.

But, Bel, you will protest, that is asking too much of your audience, for a player does not merely announce from the pianoforte the title of her ballad and expect her audience to supply the melody. Therefore, Tom, you shall have your family dinner—every note: how all remarked each other's handsomeness in muslins and coats not seen since Sunday last; with what difficulties and "pardon me's" each found his way to the seat he has occupied a score of times this year or more; how Aunt Margaret apologized for the faults of each dish until every morsel had been consumed; how general was the sentiment against the Turks;

how unwilling to tolerate such accord were our
young cousins, Will the Whig and James the dem-
ocrat, who must frequently introduce the word
"corn"; how Richard then felt impelled to dis-
course on the late agricultural decline of England
and its ill effects on the health and morality of the
people; how futile were Mother's efforts to introduce a new topic; and how at last we were spared
a further enlargement of Richard's theme by the
timely intrusion of three dogs and five cousins not
yet considered civil enough to grace the table.

There, nothing of the picture has been omitted
except your own good sense and wit and a
hymn to Aunt's custard. Truly we ought to lure
the Turks to our shores and offer them Aunt
Margaret's custard. One taste is as fatal as that of
the famed Lotos. The Turks, with their wicked
scimitars, will hire out as sedge-cutters, and you,
Tom, will be promoted to captain for bringing
about such a defeat of our enemy.

Now, dear Tom, the day beckons. I mean to
admire a cloud of blue speedwell on your favorite bank and pick a bough of hawthorn for you.
And lest you think Hampshire entirely without
event, Father tells us the Earl of Haverly, who
owns vast estates in Derbyshire, has bought
Courtland Manor and the Lower Ashe, *our Ashe*.
Shall we dare to fish our dear stream again?

Everyone sends love.

> Your affectionate sister,
> Isabel

1
❦❦❦❦❦❦❦❦❦❦

I F, AS THE great Walton himself once suggested, "Hampshire exceeds all England for swift, shallow, clear, pleasant brooks, and plenty of trout," the villagers of Ashecombe might be pardoned for supposing he could mean no other than their own Ashe.

Early one May morning not far from the banks of this superior river, where a track emerged from the hedge to make a sort of rural crossroads, a party of fishermen halted and began to quarrel.

"Fish the Upper? That trickle! Bel, you can't mean it! No Shaw fishes the Upper." The speaker, a sturdy youth of fourteen with wheaten curls above dark, straight brows and fierce blue eyes, spoke from the opening in the hedge. At his hip a basket swung loosely with the brisk rhythm of his just-halted stride. A panting, butter-colored dog dropped obediently at the boy's feet. Taking the boy's side at once were three other youths, two cast in the same fair and sturdy mold, and one, a shade more slim, with hair as dark as his brows.

From across the lane, the young woman addressed as Bel regarded the four male faces set against hers. There was directness in the straight dark brows, passion in the changeable blue eyes, insouciance and rebellion in the fine, tip-tilted noses, and resolve in the slim, squared jaws, each chin with just a hint of a stubborn point. It was the Shaw countenance, repeated with only slight variations in the faces of a score or more siblings and cousins.

Bel, her sister Diana, and her niece Sarah from their side of the lane might truly have been looking into a glass. For though the girls wore muslins and bonnets and though they were fairer and more delicate than their brothers and cousins, the stubborn point was quite as plain in the female Shaw countenance as in the male. The only male Shaw who could be said to take Bel's side in the argument was a child of four, who rode on her hip.

"I generally mean what I say, Auggie," Bel replied to the brother who had spoken.

"But, Bel," protested the tallest Shaw, her cousin Phil, "we could flog the Upper all day and never pull out a trout as big as ... as ... your shoe."

"Nevertheless, Phil," she said in the level tones of one quite used to managing her younger relatives, "we Shaws no longer have any right to fish the Lower. At least not until Papa makes the acquaintance of the earl and gains his permission."

"But the earl isn't here yet, Bel," argued Arthur, the dark-haired youth. "And since he's not arrived yet, perhaps we could fish the Lower just one last time, as a sort of farewell."

"Listen to Arthur, Bel," pleaded Phil. "The earl could not be in Ashecombe yet, or some Shaw would have seen him and we'd know. And if he's not here, he can't mind what we do."

Bel tightened her hold on the squirming child at her hip. "What's an earl?" the little one asked.

"An earl," said Auggie petulantly, "is a gouty old fellow with a dozen servants to order around who cares no more than Bel does if he spoils our sport."

"Bel doesn't mean to spoil your sport," said Diana, the taller of the slim, fair girls at Bel's side.

"Doesn't she though," retorted Auggie. "Bel always comes the big sister whenever there's sport to be had." With one booted toe he pried a stone out of the mud and kicked it into the hedge.

"Auggie Shaw," returned Diana, "you're a mean-spirited clodpole to blame Bel. Papa *told* us we wouldn't be able to fish the Lower when the earl bought Courtland."

Bel put a warning hand on her younger sister's shoulder. Diana, at twelve, was just discovering the power of a sharp tongue and was apt to goad the rebellious Auggie into real foolishness. At twenty Bel was well-acquainted with the intractability of her male relations when their mothers or sisters made suggestions as to proper behavior.

"It is a shame," she said slowly, "that we Shaws should have to forego the pleasures of our Ashe just because some stranger has been so uncivil as to buy Courtland Manor. Why do you suppose a grand, titled gentleman has purchased such an ancient pile?" She lowered her young nephew to the ground and directed him to his cousin Joe, who had so far remained silent, absorbed in arranging the moss in a pail that held several wriggling specimens of worm.

"I hadn't thought of that," said Arthur, tilting his dark head to one side. "You don't suppose, Bel, that he bought the place for the river itself?"

"No, she doesn't," said Auggie, "and she's just trying tactics on us, which for all the supposed powers locked in your brainbox, Artie, you never see."

"Auggie," said Phil, "just because *you* never think, don't go knocking Arthur. This earl, whoever he is, must have wanted something more than that old ruin—right, Arthur?"

"There you go," said Auggie, "you see how she does it. You're not even on my side anymore. Oh, why'd I get stuck with Bel for a sister? If Tom were here, he'd take us down the Lower, I know he would." He turned and flayed the unoffending hedge with the rod he held in one hand.

Bel had the lowering thought that perhaps Auggie was right, that she was losing her sense of daring and fun. She had always thought herself Tom's equal in adventure, but with Tom away she had to acknowledge that she had become quite sedate. She had spent more time instructing her brothers in the schoolroom than adventuring with them along the banks of the Ashe.

The sound of a horse bearing down upon them made the older Shaws turn and edge back from the center of the lane. Bel scooped up her nephew once again. A gentleman on a fine chestnut stallion appeared at the turning. The rider cantered his animal into the midst of their party before he reined in. Even then he allowed his restive horse to dance a bit so that Bel and her charges were compelled to flatten themselves against the sharp branches of the hedge.

Checking his horse at last, the gentleman drawled, "Good morning, Bel." He doffed his high crowned beaver and swept her a bow from his waist. His gaze took in the whole party and returned to Bel. "Surrounded by admirers, I see."

"Hah!" snorted Auggie.

"What? Contention among the Shaws?" mocked the rider.

Bel regarded his smug, handsome face with annoyance. The squire's son was Tom's friend, and Tom had always been quick to point out Darlington's good points—his green eyes and golden hair, his manly proportions, his daring as a rider, his love of sport, his willingness to laugh. But since Tom had joined the navy, Bel found it difficult to appreciate Mr. Darlington's virtues, and his assurance regularly threatened to ignite her temper. She wished he would ride on.

"Good morning, Mr. Darlington," she said.

"*Darling* to you, Bel," he whispered, leaning down and stroking her cheek with one finger. Backed against the hedge and holding the child, she could not evade the unwelcome familiarity.

"Leave off, Darlington," said Arthur quietly.

"Of course, if you say so, Master Arthur," the gentleman returned, straightening. "Not headed for the Lower, are you, Auggie?" he inquired of the younger boy. "Sad misfortune for the Shaws, isn't it? Can't treat the Lower Ashe as your private river any longer, can you?"

"Has this earl actually arrived at Courtland, Darlington?" asked Phil.

"Arrives today, I hear. His man's there already, though—on the lookout for poachers on the Lower, I'm sure," replied Darlington.

"Well, that won't concern us, Mr. Darlington," said Bel. "We shall do our fishing today on the Upper."

"Trout, Bel? On the Upper?" Darlington paused and seemed to consider the idea. "I doubt it. Easier to catch a husband, Bel."

"If I wanted one."

"You want one, Aunt Bel, Cousin Bel, Sister Bel." It was the sort of comment Darlington liked to taunt her with, reminding her that for nearly four years she had been playmate, nursemaid, and governess to nearly a dozen younger Shaws.

"I am quite content to be of service to my family, Mr. Darlington."

"Oh, Bel," said Darlington, "I love you when you're haughty."

"I think not."

"Believe what you like, Bel, but you will marry me." Once again Darlington leaned down to touch her cheek and whispered for her alone, "All the Shaws depend on you to make their fortunes." She thought he meant to kiss her in front of them all, but he pulled back abruptly.

"What the devil!" he exclaimed, and his startled

horse reared, forcing him to grab the animal's mane to keep his seat.

Then Bel could see the source of his consternation. On the other side of the hedge, Mr. Darlington's hat was bobbing away, as if it had suddenly sprouted wings. Bel glanced at the boys across the lane. Phil and Joe and Arthur stood smiling blandly at Darlington, but Auggie had vanished.

"The devil take you, Auggie Shaw," yelled Darlington, and dug his spurs into his horse. The chestnut surged down the lane.

"Auntie Bel," said the little one in her arms, "is that man angry because Uncle Auggie stole his hat?"

"Oh, yes, Kit," said Bel. Then she looked at the three other boys. The blue Shaw eyes were bright with mirth, and it was quite fatal to her dignity to meet those gazes. Whoops of laughter took them all. Darlington, trapped in the narrow lane, rode repeatedly against the hedge, leaning out to snatch the hat, pulling back empty-handed to keep his seat. But as Darlington gained on the bobbing hat on the far side of the hedge, Bel collected herself.

"Oh, dear! Phil, Arthur, Joe, girls, Darlington will be in a rage when he catches up with Auggie. Hurry!" They grabbed the pail and their baskets and rods and scrambled through the break in the hedge.

From the top of a low rise they looked back to see Darlington, his hat on his head once more, cantering toward the narrow opening in the hedge, and Auggie, on their side of the hedge, striding across the open field, poking the air with his fishing rod in a triumphant imitation of the trick he had played on Darlington. The dog, Honey, leapt and barked at the boy's side, apparently sharing the triumph.

Darlington reined in at the break in the hedge and shouted out, "Bel Shaw, you'll pay for your brother's insult, I promise you. Nobody makes a mock of Alan Darlington."

The angry words hung in the still air and seemed to silence even the birds. The younger Shaws looked quietly at Bel. Below them Darlington rode off.

"How'd you like that, Bel?" asked Auggie, coming up to them, panting. "I put Darlington in his place for you, didn't I?"

"That you did," said Bel. "Thank you, Auggie." The boy was grinning with self-satisfaction, and Bel could see that this was no time to comment on the likely results of his prank. She looked at the worried faces of the others. "Let's not worry about Darlington," she said. "It's time and enough that we started fishing."

"Bel," said Arthur, "we don't really have to fish the Upper, do we? Not today?"

"Couldn't we go to the Lower one last time?" asked Phil.

"Before Fanny and Louisa come and spoil our summer?" It was Diana who made this last plea, and it was a powerful one, for their rich London cousins were the most tiresome of summer guests.

A half dozen pairs of sober blue eyes pleaded with Bel to restore the pleasure of the day. Her own girlhood summers on the Ashe were gone, had ended with Tom's leaving and her assumption of the duties of eldest child, but at least she had had them in full measure. What harm could there be in one last expedition to their favorite spot?

"Very well," she said. "To the Lower Ashe, Shaws."

"Hurrah for Bel!" shouted Auggie.

2

A N IMPERTINENT BEAM of sunlight, no respecter of rank or wealth, penetrated the curtained darkness where Nicholas Arthur Seymour, the Earl of Haverly, lay. The saucy beam danced a little with the gentle movement of the trees through which it fell, and played lightly over the earl's closed lids with their fringe of black lashes. At the touch he woke, sat up, threw the covers off his lean frame, and pushed aside the heavy bed hangings.

Dappled sunlight shimmered whitely on the bare wood floor, and sparkling dust motes swirled in the currents created by his sudden movement. Birdsong from the trees beyond his window seemed to have reached symphonic proportions. His head throbbed, and he lifted a strong, fine-boned hand to cover his eyes. He felt as if he had only just that moment dozed off. The night's restless dreams had wearied him more than the long journey he had undertaken the day before.

He pulled the rumpled, sweat-dampened nightshirt over his head, and tossed it behind him on the bed. The cold air in the unheated chamber raised goose pimples on his arms and chest, but the chill was welcome after the hot stickiness with which he had awakened too often in London. He had been a fool to think London, with its gay crowds, its laughter and music and light spilling into the night streets,

10

its thousand temptations, was any place for him. He had believed that all the years in his uncle's well-regimented house had made him indifferent to the rustle of silks, the curve and sway of hips, the swell of a white breast above a bit of lace. He had been wrong. If he were not so certain that his parents were in hell, he would be tempted to wish them there himself.

But in the country he would sleep well, he was sure. A day of fishing his own stream, on his own land, would cure the restlessness that had plagued him in town. He stood and stretched, brushing with his fingertips the top of the bed frame and disturbing a small cloud of dust. He sneezed. Maybe he would consent to hire a housekeeper after all.

He glanced around the unfamiliar room. In the daylight he could see that Peter Farre had not misrepresented Courtland Manor's state of decay, and that pleased him. Other than the bed with its faded grandeur, the room was bare. Unfurnished, it was more fully his, and there would be time enough to furnish it after the fishing season ended. He strode in the direction of an open door through which he could see the valise he'd brought with him from town.

The dressing room was brighter than the bedchamber, and he blinked. Apparently he had slept away the early rise, the day's best fishing. Farre would answer for that. No doubt the old curmudgeon had already been to the river, *Nick's* river. He pulled the few items he needed from the valise—smalls, stockings, and dark breeches. Drawing these on, he looked round for his shaving things. There they were, laid out for him, another sign of the contrary Farre.

When Nick, at seventeen, had first come to his uncle's Haverly estate, he had concluded that all the servants there were mad or so shaped by his uncle's caprices that their eccentricities approached madness.

All but Farre. He was not mad, just maddening, determined to be the servant only when it suited him. After his Uncle Miles' death Nick had left the lot of them behind, provided for and charged with the task of maintaining his uncle's great house as the museum it had become years before the man died. But he had taken Farre with him. It had been Farre's description of the Ashe that had induced Nick to buy Courtland Manor. Here, Nick would make a place for them. Farre would have his stable, and Nick his library, and they would fish the summer away, untroubled by the past.

Nick dipped his brush in a basin of icy water and began to work up a lather in the soap cup. The river beckoned, and in his haste to get to it, he nicked himself under the chin. He toweled off, pulled on an old shirt and jacket, jammed his feet into his cold boots, and returned to the bedroom. He rummaged in the bedclothes until he found his Walter Scott and stuffed the worn volume in his coat pocket. As he descended the stairs, he thought to run his hands through his black hair once.

He found Farre in the stable, pulling a mound of moldy straw into the wide center aisle between the stalls. The floor was cambered, forming two gullies for drainage, and it was plain that the sagging roof had let in rain all spring. Little had been done to protect tools or wood from the elements. Harness, carts, rakes, and an old box for cutting chaff lay in rusty disarray in one corner. Farre, who had kept Nick's uncle's vast stable clean and well-ordered, with a corps of boys to help him, had made some sacrifice on Nick's account to have accepted this ruin.

Nick studied his friend. Farre had stripped to his shirtsleeves, and a film of sweat glazed his balding brow as he worked. Farre had altered in the eleven years of their aquaintance. The once-red hair was white and thin, revealing a wide brow and large ears.

The skin, too, seemed thin, the bones of the cheeks and the sharp bridge of the nose apparent. Farre seemed pared down to a wiry energetic frame of a man. Nick looked for another tool, found a pitchfork, and began to scoop straw from an adjoining stall onto the pile.

"Decided to get up, did you," said his companion. He cast Nick a look that plainly reproved every hasty detail of Nick's dress and person.

"No thanks to you," Nick replied. "We missed the early rise."

"Would have in any case. Stalls needed cleaning. Couldn't leave the horses to stand in this muck all day."

"I would have helped," said Nick.

"A fine thing for your *lordship* to be doing."

Nick straightened and leaned on his pitchfork. "I thought we agreed you wouldn't plague me with ceremony."

"We agreed you'd give town life a try, too," said his companion.

Nick shrugged his shoulders and hefted his pitchfork again. "I did. I'm not cut out for it."

"Stuff! Three weeks in a hotel. Didn't even go into the Lords."

"I saw every damned sight in London, rode in the park twice a day, and was overcharged by the tailor, the boot-maker, the haberdasher, and everyone else."

"Did you talk to one member of the quality?"

"I've got no talent for self-introduction."

"Excuses, lad. Did you write those letters when your uncle died?"

"To two ancient dowagers, who probably don't go about at all? How could they have introduced me to anyone?"

"Trust me, my boy, if you had shown your face to that pair, you would have seen the inside of every drawing room in the West End."

Nick snorted. "What makes you so sure of that?"

"Turns out, Nick, my boy, that I've talked to more ladies than you have. Those ladies look out for their own, they do. A dowager, she's got a daughter, or a granddaughter, or a niece who needs a husband, and you are a prime catch."

"Nick Seymour a prime catch? Farre, you're as daft as the rest of the lot at Haverly."

The older man stopped raking. "Well, that's as may be, your lordship, but a titled gentleman with twenty thousand a year is a catch in my book."

"As I said, it's not Nick Seymour that's the catch."

"You sell yourself short, lad, you do. What is it that women want if they don't want you?"

"They want a hero."

"What? You mean some fellow out of one of your books?"

"All the heroes aren't in books. But yes, a hero, a man of action, a fellow who can handle a sword or a pistol or at least his fists." Nick made a thrust with his pitchfork.

"Stuff," said Farre. "You don't know the first thing about what women want."

"Precisely, and that proves my point. I am ignorant of women and therefore not likely to please the least discriminating of the sex." It was not entirely a lie, for he did not suppose all women to be like the women who had come to his parents' house, but he could hardly tell the truth about himself to his friend.

"Time to learn then," Farre was saying, "and I don't mean by reading all the blasted books in your library." He tapped the book in Nick's pocket with the tip of the rake handle.

"You think I should go to school then, at eight and twenty? Or hire a tutor, an instructress?"

"Now that's an idea, lad," said Farre, beginning to rake again. "Thought you might have gotten around to it in town. So set up some pretty young doxy who knows a trick or two."

"Even a mistress requires an introduction, presumably, before one can make an offer," Nick said dryly, but Farre's suggestion had surprised him.

"Then do it, lad. You can't be tangling yourself up in the sheets every night and snarling your way through the days."

"And my groom can't be telling me what to do, Farre." Nick regretted the hasty words immediately. The scratch of the rake stopped, then started again, unnaturally loud to his ears.

"Of course not ... your lordship. As if I would." The rake continued.

Some very low words came to Nick's mind, words that he had learned in his parents' house. He wielded his pitchfork in silence until Farre's movements revealed that the old man's anger was somewhat mollified. In the early days at Haverly Nick had escaped his uncle's demands by hiding in the stables to read. There Farre found him and coaxed him out into the woods and fields—Farre, who knew horses and fishing and who could teach without embarrassing his student. Nick had soon found he could talk to Farre, but every quarrel made him fear to lose this first friend. Yet he had watched and waited, learning to recognize the moment when his friend might be approached again.

Now as Farre put up the rake, Nick ventured to speak to him. "Are you still willing to fish with me?"

Farre turned and, to Nick's relief, smiled. "Aye, stubborn lad that you are."

3
€€€€€€€€€€€€

OVERGROWN AS THE property was, the path to the river led clear and straight to the brow of the hill, then wound down the hillside through the wood by a series of switchbacks. Farre was content to follow Nick at a distance, for their talk had set him thinking once again about a problem that appeared to have no solution. How was he to get the boy out among his own kind?

The boy was free of Haverly after ten years a virtual prisoner there, but there were lingering effects. A man couldn't abuse a young horse for years and expect him to be sweet-tempered for a new master. The old earl had worked hard to deaden the boy's sense of humor and to teach him to hold himself above everyone else. So here was the lad, starved for real companionship but knowing nothing about how to get it. And as Farre had guessed, that healthy young body was sending Nick nightly messages of its desires.

So what was Farre to do? The earl's pride would not allow him to mix easily with the sort of wenches who would be glad enough to instruct him, and he wasn't going to hire a mistress. Hired love spoke too much of the ways of the boy's dead parents. Rakehell and wanton, the pair had apparently been well-matched. Farre had heard enough of them from the

other servants at Haverly to know how careless and
indifferent they had been toward their only child.

Farre himself was fifty years old. Ten years before,
he had buried the sweetest, sauciest woman to fill an
apron or warm a bed, and he ached for her yet. In
her lifetime she had not given him a son, but in
dying she had set him drifting until he stopped at
Haverly, and there a tall, thin gawk of a youth had
taken to hiding in the stable loft when he could escape the big house. The boy had been a good tree-
climber, an intense listener, and so perfect in sitting
still that sometimes he had seemed made of stone.
But Farre had coaxed him to the banks of the earl's
stream and taught him to fish and then to ride and
then to do with sureness dozens of things a man
should be able to do. Lean and supple strength now
characterized the man, and Farre believed his lordship was handy enough with his fives to hold his
own against burlier opponents. But Nick still rated
himself as if he were that lanky boy. And the books
he read told him that kings and knights won the fair
maid, not quiet gentlemen who fished and read.

Farre had hoped that a stay in London would
show Nick how many men found a woman without
having to fight a duel or conquer a city on her behalf.
But Nick hadn't lasted a month in town, and now he
would bury himself on this property and Farre
wouldn't be able to budge him till the fish stopped
biting.

The scant foliage of early spring allowed glimpses
of the flashing river, and the sound of waters rose to
meet them. From the rush of it, like a chorus of whispers, Nick judged the river to be running full and
deep, and his impatience to see it grew. Sleek and
shimmering trout would be waiting there, where the
current could bring them flies and larvae.

Then another sound reached his ears—not a sound

of wood dwellers, but the sound of boys yelling, a
dog barking, and a great deal of splashing. Someone
was in his river, driving all the fish into holes and
shadows, from which even the cleverest of fishermen
would not be able to lure them.

He stared through the trees but could not see the
trespassers. Whoever they were, they had stolen his
moment of pleasure. He strode toward a tiny gravel
beach at the foot of the hill. Then he was in the open,
looking at a wide, shallow pool where the river had
carved out a bit of the facing meadow. It ran swift
and clear over pebbles and sand. Willows and reeds
bent softly down along the opposite bank that
stretched away into meadow.

Four youths in breeches splashed in the depths, a
tawny dog barking at them from a rock. Two girls sat
decorously on a second rock, plaiting reeds, and a
mere child, not much out of leading strings, threw
pebbles into the shallows. In their midst was a young
woman in white muslin, her head tilted down so that
Nick could see only the top of her bonnet, her attitude serene and reflective in spite of the noise around
her. The sun was so bright on her muslin dress that
her skirts seemed to burn with white light. The
young woman's hands were at her side, holding the
skirts of her dress above the water. Little wavelets
from the swimmers washed gently against her white
legs.

Nick had a sudden, futile impulse to check the momentum of his anger, but he couldn't. He dropped
the rod and gear he carried and waded into the
stream. "What are you doing in my river?" he
shouted, wishing at the same time that he had come
upon the girl silently so that he could watch her un-
observed.

At his words the girl in the middle of the pool
looked up, startled, and the splashing and shouting
stopped. Nick sensed that all the children were star-

ing at him. He felt Farre step up behind him softly and deliberately, but he couldn't look away from the face of the girl. If spring had a maiden's face, it was this face, all blossoms of hawthorn and eyes of blue speedwell and curls as gold as honeysuckle.

Bel looked toward the angry voice. She had been watching a school of silver minnows at her feet, and, looking up suddenly, she was momentarily blinded by the water's glare. Then she saw the man. He looked not much older than she and was dressed like a shepherd—such a shepherd as Paris must have been when the contending goddesses asked him to judge their beauty. Even anger couldn't mar his face, fine and lean, and oddly, she thought, suffused with wonder.

"Your river? Who are you?" she asked the shepherd.

"I am Nicholas Seymour," he said.

Darlington's warning came back to her, and she feared she had landed them all in the briers. "I suppose you are the earl's man come to clear the way for him," she said. There was nothing for it but to apologize and take themselves off before he inquired too closely into their actions. "I assure you we mean no harm. Until now this stretch of the Ashe has been ours to f—enjoy, and we came to say farewell to our favorite places before the earl arrives. Pardon us, please. We will gather our things and be gone, and your master will never be the wiser."

"I am not the earl's man," said Nick, annoyed by the girl's mistaking him for a servant and unready for their conversation to end. "*I* am Haverly, and by your own admission you are trespassers. Do you not know I can bring you up before the magistrate for such an act?"

Haverly. Bel paused to adjust her thinking. The Earl of Haverly was this . . . rude young man? "And would you, my lord, bring such as these before the law for their enjoyment of your river?" She gestured with a broad sweep of her arm at the children, who stood still as statues. Even the dog appeared cowed.

"Wouldn't I though. Don't think to excuse your intrusion by citing their innocence. You must see that you and your trespassing band of urchins have spoiled the fishing this day." There was a burst of laughter from one of the boys, and Nick turned to them. They stood in the steam, water dripping from their heads, rivulets gleaming on their arms and chests. Four pairs of blue eyes glared at him without any apparent fear of the law.

When he turned back to the girl, he saw beyond her on the opposite bank the rods and baskets and nets the trespassers had with them. "You're poachers, too, aren't you?" He looked at the boys again. The slim, dark-haired boy who reminded Nick of himself had the grace to look abashed, but the others appeared as maddeningly unimpressed with his power and position as the girl.

"You may think us poachers," said the girl, drawing Nick's attention back to her, "but you can hardly prove it."

"Then you'll show me what's in that net you've got anchored in the stream," Nick said.

The girl's eyes darkened, and she let her skirts fall into the water. "Certainly. Auggie," she said to the sturdiest, most sullen-looking of the boys, "show his lordship your net."

"But, Bel," the boy began.

"Do it," she ordered curtly.

The boy waded across the stream reluctantly, his long, angry strides sending ripples in every direction. Defiantly he seized the net and lifted it out of the shaded pool where it lay.

Inside gleamed four of the prettiest trout Nick had seen in a long time. He waded into the stream past the staring boys and the angry girl. As he passed her, he caught the scent of lavender.

"Not poachers?" he said, snatching the dripping net from the boy. "Still, it's a wonder such an unruly lot managed to take these fish."

The girl turned on him, and he found he couldn't move. He felt the stream's icy swirl at his knees, but his skin felt heated as if with a fever. "Tell me, your lordship," she was asking, "precisely which portion of the river do you own?"

He didn't think she realized how close they stood. The stream tangled her skirts about her calves, and Nick had a sudden recollection of white sheets tangled about his own limbs. He felt a queer sinking sensation in the pit of his stomach that made it hard to think.

"All the river from one end of Courtland to the other," he managed.

"So you own all the water in this pond?"

"Yes, of course, and what's more, Miss Rag Manners, all the fish."

"Though this morning this same water must have been Farmer Elworthy's, and this evening, perforce, it must become the squire's? Unless you can command the stream."

"Your logic only makes you the more guilty, ma'am, since you must have realized what you were about when you brought these children here and led them in crime."

"Crime! You accuse *us* of crime?"

The girl's outraged hauteur only angered Nick more. She seemed to think he was the offending party. "It is my right and mine alone to take from these waters whatever luckless trout happen to swim in them, and I'll have these fish, wherever you claim to have taken them." He hefted the net with its gleaming catch and started back across the pond.

Standing so close to the girl made his mind sluggish and his limbs weak.

"I hardly think your lordship can claim proprietorship over every trout that swims in the Ashe, and you cannot say with certainty whether these four came from your portion of the river or from another."

Nick stopped and looked at her. "Then perhaps you should take me to court, ma'am."

Bel hardly knew what overcame her in that moment. It was unreasonable to expect a mere stranger to understand the insult he had offered her family, but then she supposed he was the sort of man who held himself above his neighbors whoever they were.

"You provoking, rude, arrogant man! You're so puffed up in your own conceit that you cannot excuse a small trespass in the name of neighborliness. You might have welcomed these boys in friendship and let them in turn show you all they know of the river, for they know it well and can pull out a like catch any day they choose. Now—"

"They'd better not," interrupted Nick. "This is my land now. Disturb my peace again, drop one line into this stretch of the Ashe again, and I will have you up before the magistrate that very day."

"Very well," said the lady. She turned away and called to her charges, who came to her side in silence. While the boys pulled on shirts and jackets, the girl swung the child up onto a rock, dried his feet, and helped him into his shoes, heedless of her own damp gown. When the others had been attended to, she turned her back, squeezed out her skirts, and pulled on her own stockings and shoes.

Nick found he could not look away from this procedure though he could see little more than her angry back and her frowning relations. A few quick motions and the girl stood. She took the child in her arms, and sent the others off along the far shore.

Above the pond where the river narrowed, a great low branch looped across the stream, making a natural bridge. The tallest boy took charge helping them all across. When they reached Nick's side of the river, the girl turned back to him one last time.

"My lord," she said, "we have been remiss in introductions. We are the Shaws, you see." She said it as if she were proclaiming them royalty. "It will certainly interest Mr. Augustus Shaw, the magistrate, to hear what you have to say against his children and grandchildren. Good day."

She turned away, and the little band of children disappeared around the hill. But the voice of the youngest came back. "Was that man the earl, Auntie Bel?"

"Yes, Kit, he was," came the reply.

"But he's not old and gouty as Auggie told us."

"No," said the girl's voice, "but he is rude and haughty."

"Is that worse?" asked the child.

"Much worse," said the girl. Nick heard the confirming laughter of the others at her tone.

"He'll hear us, Bel," said another voice in warning.

"Let him hear."

Suddenly Nick was aware of Farre behind him, a witness to the whole encounter. He returned to the wooded edge of the stream and lowered the holding net into the cool water, anchoring it in place with a few stones.

"Farre," he said, "don't say a thing."

"Wouldn't dream of it, lad," said his companion cheerfully. Nick felt a light touch on his shoulder. Then Farre spoke again. "Beauties, aren't they. Wager you those boys never took that lot out of this hole."

Nick looked at the wide shallow pool that seemed so empty now that the Shaws were gone. He had routed the intruders. Why did he feel as if he'd lost a battle? "There's not a trout will rise again today after the commotion they made. I'll be lucky to get a fish this week."

"Nay, lad. You'll get one this afternoon, though I don't know how many we can eat. Come along. Let's see if we can find where the Shaws poached from you."

"Damn, I'm a fool," said Nick.

Farre laughed. "That may be lad, but at least you introduced yourself to a lady."

Monday evening

Dear Tom,

We have met the Earl of Haverly, though I must confess our introduction was not what Mama might have wished.

Having a perfect day and good information that the earl had not yet arrived in Ashecombe, we dared to fish the Lower. Remember that Fanny and Louisa will descend upon us soon to spoil our summer, and forgive us for taking the risk. Auggie assures me you would have done the same.

The earl and a servant came upon us at the low pool just around the bend from the water-wheel. You know the place. You will hardly credit the insults the earl offered us or his arrogance in claiming the Ashe as his own. He threatened in the end to bring us before the magistrate, and you may imagine my satisfaction in telling him our connection to that person.

But, Bel, you will say, could you not find a way to make him welcome and win his friendship? I can only say that he is not what anyone expected and that one cannot welcome in friendship a man who begins by accusing one of misconduct. He used the word "crime" and suggested that I had led my innocent charges into poaching.

The worst of it is I have not the courage to approach Papa as he has weightier matters on his mind, what with the poor folk from Hilcombe coming to trial. He must be told, I suppose, before he attempts to make the earl's acquaintance, but I do not think they will soon meet as the earl is most high-handed and unlikely to take an interest in the neighborhood.

Auggie is hot for revenge, though Arthur and I have tried to dissuade him from such schemes as damming the Ashe at Eldon Barrow or loosing otters along the earl's banks. Still, I think revenge a most satisfying object of contemplation. The haughty earl should be forced to endure a Shaw dinner, he should be subjected to the toad-eating of Louisa and Fanny, he should face you in a regular mill and learn what it is to insult the Shaws. Trust me to think of some just retribution in your absence.

As ever,
Isabel

4

A WET, GUSTY STORM following close on the heels of
Bel's meeting with the earl confined the younger
Shaws to the schoolroom for three days, until at last
it blew itself out, leaving shining tracks on all the
lanes. Bel pulled a faded red pelisse about her shoulders, strapped on her pattens, and escaped.

Despite her teasing letter to Tom, she had dismissed revenge as a petty desire entirely unworthy of
Miss Shaw of Shaw House. But a vengeful spirit had
wedged itself firmly into some corner of her mind,
refusing to be dislodged by the charades and conun-
drums, spillikins and paper cutouts with which she
had occupied her siblings. It had not helped that
Auggie referred sullenly and often to the fish he regarded as stolen from him by the earl. Even her parents' company could not distract her. Augustus and
Serena Shaw had been absorbed in reviewing the evidence against a group of villagers who were accused
of machine-wrecking.

At the height of the storm, the earl's man had arrived, evoking a flurry of hospitality which died
abruptly when the man requested that Augustus
Shaw come before the earl with an account of his
stewardship of the Courtland estate. The vengeful
spirit in Bel's mind had stirred restlessly.

She had found no opportunity to tell her father
about the unfortunate meeting of his children and

new neighbor, and it seemed the haughty earl was demanding her father's records because of her own folly. In defying the earl, she had exposed her father, the soul of integrity, to a stranger's scrutiny and censure.

Her father did not reveal the outcome of his meeting with the earl, but returned to his contemplation of the affairs of the poor accused villagers as if there had been no lordly summons from their arrogant neighbor. Only the little voice that whispered vengeance in Bel's ear would not be stilled. It had made her laugh, really. What could she do to the man?

Retreating clouds were spitting a few isolated drops of rain as she made her way along the drive. From the road she paused to look back at the house, shaking her head at such reflections. Contemplating with relish the humiliation of a peer of the realm was not at all the thing for the daughter of such a house to be doing. If Shaw House was not in the guidebooks, it deserved to be. It had a handsome gray stucco front with regularly spaced white casement windows across the wide upper story. Tall windows at the ends of the two protruding wings of the lower story hinted at the size and loftiness of the interior apartments. Four white columns lifted a pediment above the door with restrained and unpretentious dignity. Elms of great age and grandeur sheltered the rear of the house, and a vast green park swept from the door to the road. In short, every feature reflected the dignity and honor of the Shaws themselves.

When travelers inquired about it, as they inevitably did, Mrs. Jenner, the housekeeper, would be quick to offer refreshment and a tour of the principal rooms. And Mr. Jenner, the butler, would be as ready to tell the story of Colonel Shaw, a soldier of considerable courage in the service of the Bonnie Prince.

Every Shaw knew the story. The colonel had expressed in the hearing of his restored sovereign the view that next to serving the crown in yet another war nothing could be so satisfying as casting his line upon a swift-running stream. Not too many years later his amused and grateful liege had settled upon the retiring soldier the large languishing estate of a man who had backed Cromwell. The colonel, in spite of his professed desire to do nothing more than fish, soon busied himself in building a house, getting a family, and improving the land he had been given.

Jenner would content himself with these revelations, of course. Pride would permit no reference to the hard times upon which the Shaws had fallen. Should the travelers inquire as to the precise acreage of the estate, Jenner would cough discreetly. There would be no need to point out that the original estate was now divided among three brothers and a son, that the Shaws had become as numerous as the rooms in their gracious home, or that dowries and settlements divided among so many for so long had shrunk to humble proportions hardly worthy of the grandeur of such a fine old house.

Bel turned toward the village, intending to lose the dismals in exercise and the beauty of the day. Ashecombe, with its three substantial dwellings, its dozen shops, fifteen cottages, inn, and church, straddled the river two miles below Shaw House. Even in the awkward pattens she soon reached the stone bridge, where a deep turn in the river separated the broad, flat reaches of meadow and field through which the Upper Ashe flowed from the deeper stretches of the Lower Ashe where it curved past the church and vicarage, Mr. Elworthy's farm, Courtland Manor, and Squire Darlington's land.

Once again her thoughts fixed on the earl's contempt for her and her family. She gazed from the bridge at the rain-swollen Ashe rushing to the deep pools that made the banks of Courtland Manor so inviting to fishermen. How maddening that she could not put the man out of her mind. His sudden appearance at the edge of the stream had been like an episode out of the oldest tales—Hermes appearing before Kalypso, Apollo before Daphne, a god descending to earth in shepherd's guise. Then, of course, the god had spoken, as rudely as any mortal Bel had ever encountered. Would that she could snub him as he deserved.

Such feelings were not much relieved by hearing that general sentiment in the village ran in the earl's favor. It was but a few steps from the linen draper's to the butcher's, yet on the way Bel had to endure the earl's praises sung in half a dozen different keys. Apparently his man was interviewing candidates for several posts at Courtland, and everyone in Ashecombe with a brother, sister, or cousin in need of a situation was full of wonder at the wages that had been mentioned.

To hear the villagers talk, Haverly's coming to Ashecombe was as prodigious and wonderful an event as the arrival of a royal personage and much more likely to bring prosperity to all. It was a shame that the earl was not about to hear himself so universally praised. The toadying of his neighbors would no doubt suit his sense of consequence. Interrupting the butcher's further encomiums on the earl's generosity as an employer, Bel completed the order her mother had requested and made her escape.

Outside the butcher's door, however, she came face-to-face with Mrs. Nye, a widow whose feelings were most likely contrary to her own. Dedicated equally to the ill of the parish and to gossip, Mrs. Nye would be sure to have something to say about Lord Haverly.

"Oh, good morning, Miss Shaw. Will you be so good as to give me your arm to cross the road?" asked Mrs. Nye. Bel complied, shifting her basket and steadying the older woman with a firm hand under one frail elbow.

Some years earlier after escorting Mrs. Nye about the village for most of a long July afternoon, Tom had unkindly but accurately dubbed the old woman "Echo." It was true that Mrs. Nye had wasted away with the years until little was left of her once-substantial person except a great deal of white hair and a shrill, many-noted voice. Still, she reminded Bel less of the classical nymph than of a determined bird singing steadily from the hedge to a stream of indifferent passersby.

"How do you like this earl settling among us?" Mrs. Nye began. "It is a great good fortune, is it not? Especially for all the Shaw girls. A single man must rely on the resources of the neighborhood for his entertainment, of course. I daresay one will meet him at dinners throughout the summer. You and your cousins will find yourselves in a much enlarged circle, to be sure. Not that you, Miss Shaw, must seek a suitor when Mr. Darlington has set his cap, but your cousin Ellen and your fine London cousins must profit."

"Everyone in Ashecombe seems eager to profit, Mrs. Nye, but I hardly think our new neighbor will enlarge his circle to include the Shaws," said Bel, helping her companion around a deep rut in the road.

"I expect the earl will give a ball, don't you, once he has Courtland Manor restored, of course," confided Mrs. Nye, as if Bel had not spoken at all. "You do know that he means to restore Courtland." Mrs. Nye went on to describe the extent of the earl's fortune and properties in Derbyshire.

Bel was amazed at the grand edifice of hopes and schemes her neighbors were building on the slight foundation of the earl's purchase of an old ruin. He was no more than a rude, selfish young man, who probably meant only to fish the Ashe for a few weeks and then return to his *ton* friends, but he had offended her family and set the sensible village of Ashecombe on its ear with that supreme unconcern of the aristocrat for the villager that her Whiggish cousins decried so often. Her desire for revenge was nearly choking her as she listened to Mrs. Nye's further effusions in praise of the earl.

"Mrs. Nye, even if Lord Haverly restores Courtland, he is so ill—" She stopped herself from commenting further on his manners. She could not very well do so without revealing her encounter with the earl. And to reveal it to Mrs. Nye was to reveal it to all of Ashecombe.

Mrs. Nye halted and paled at the words. "Ill—the earl ill? It's not grave, is it, Miss Shaw?"

Suddenly, Bel perceived a means of revenge so simple, so neat, so unexpectedly available to her that she could not allow the opportunity to pass her by. She would not hesitate as Hamlet had but avenge her father at once.

"It does not appear so," she said slowly, gently urging Mrs. Nye forward again. "It is only a . . . fever, after all. He must have attempted the Ashe, and you know, Mrs. Nye, how hazardous to one's health it is to stand all day in a chill stream. I have no doubt that Lord Haverly will be well soon if . . . he receives proper care." She paused. They were now nearly across the road. "But, of course, he has no servants about, does he? And no female member of his household, and we all know what men are in such a situation. Perhaps you should take him some of your calf's-foot jelly, Mrs. Nye?"

"Oh, I will," breathed Mrs. Nye solemnly, "and Mrs. Elworthy will want to take him some lavender water."

"Oh, yes, we must *all* be neighborly, don't you think?" urged Bel, struggling to maintain a grave countenance.

Mrs. Nye said nothing for once. Her eyes moved rapidly back and forth as if her thinking had outstripped her powers of speech. She seemed to forget Bel's presence and turned away, leaving the assistance of Bel's arm. What visions of fatal disease and restorative ministrations had seized the woman's imagination Bel did not know, but further down the street Mrs. Nye apparently recovered enough to speak to Mrs. Pence. Bel smiled and turned homeward with light steps.

Vulgar curiosity about the earl would never lead any of his lesser neighbors to disturb his peace, but solicitude for his health would bring all of Ashecombe to his door. Bel could see the scene: the haughty earl and his man receiving call after call as each of their neighbors brought some remedy or other for the earl's imaginary ills and perhaps something for his conceit. She hoped someone would bring him leeches.

5
❧❧❧❧❧❧❧❧❧❧❧

WITH THE LATE afternoon sun slanting in long shafts past the library windows, Nick pulled his chair closer to the fire and stretched his legs toward the fender, propping his crossed ankles where the flames' heat could warm his toes. He had put aside Augustus Shaw's ledgers. The man was more than honest. He had clearly been resourceful and generous in his management of the property. Nick had spent the day riding about Courtland, seeing for himself just what the ledgers had told him he would find—tenants in roomy, well-tended cottages, land in good heart, modern drainage, sensible enclosures with enough common land remaining for the people to graze a cow or two of their own. How it had been managed was all there in the accounts. Antiquities and furnishings from the manor house had been sold off as allowed in the terms of the will, and monies had been invested, little by little, in a series of well-conceived improvements.

Nick's Uncle Miles would never have dreamed of such a sacrifice of the lord's house, yet of the lessons Nick had learned from his Uncle Miles those pertaining to the management of an earl's house and lands had been at first the most satisfying. In his first months at Haverly, under the guise of learning what his station in life was to require of him, Nick had opened the great ledgers again and again to the roll of servants and their wages, the list of tenants and their rents. The sums alone had been magnificent, but more wonderful still had been the regularity. Quarter by quarter the butler, the housekeeper, Farre, the stable hands, the footmen, and the cook had received their wages. Even the lowliest laundress, Grace Simpton, had been there, her four pounds per quarter duly recorded.

In his parents' household, what servants there were had come and gone with bewildering rapidity. Nick had been ten before he perfectly understood that the servants expected to be paid, resented it when they were not, and were inclined to take a bit of plate or silver with them to cover any losses incurred in the service of the Seymours.

But such lessons had not been on his mind when rain had made a sieve of the Courtland stable roof. In those moments of shifting horses, gear, and hay to protected corners of the old building, Nick had been cursing the Shaws. The encounter at the river still rankled, and he did not hesitate to lay the blame for the disrepair of his property on the man who had managed it for fifteen years. After all, if the children were not above poaching from the estate, what depredations was the man himself guilty of? Nick had insisted on seeing the ledgers that day.

Farre, assuming his most distant manner, had said, "Yes, your lordship," and "No, your lordship," and ridden to do Nick's bidding.

But with the appearance of Mr. Shaw, Nick had immediately forgotten the ledgers. As tall as Nick, of an age with Farre, Mr. Shaw entered Courtland Manor like a lion, shaking his bright, wild hair about his fiercely genial and vivid face. On Nick he leveled a gaze as warm and direct as a shaft of sunlight, in which Nick could detect no defensiveness at being called to account, as there might have been in a man who had abused his trust, nor any resentment, as there might have been in a man who had done his job well.

"So your stable's giving you a bit of trouble," said Mr. Shaw. "Do you mind if I take a look?"

A very few of Mr. Shaw's forceful strides brought them across the gravel drive to the damp stable. There they walked back and forth, examining the dripping timbers and the roof itself. At Mr. Shaw's insistence they mounted a ladder to examine the very framework of crucks and braces. Nick, arguing that certain of the timbers must be replaced, was surprised to find his new neighbor agreeing with him and offering the names of several craftsmen in the valley who could be relied upon to restore the roof properly.

The visit of Mr. Shaw had left him thinking about Bel Shaw—that is, more than he had been thinking of her. A dozen times a day fragments of their conversation at the river came back to him, and he would imagine himself saying quite different things to her. Once, staring at the rain-swollen Ashe, he had imagined himself snatching her up in his arms as the river's waters threatened to wash her away. The image had a hold on him he could not shake.

Carriage wheels crunching to a halt on the gravel of the drive broke his reverie. He heard voices and a shuffle of footsteps along the walk. Fleetingly, he regretted that no housekeeper or servant had yet been hired. Farre, at work in the stable, would not answer the door, and Nick would have to leave the visitors standing or answer himself. He had his boots off, too. He jammed them on his feet and strode to the door, reaching it as the fall of the knocker reverberated in the empty entry.

When he opened the door, two white-haired ladies, one on each arm of an equally aged coachmen, stood before him. Each carried a small basket. There was a brief moment in which the ladies stared at him and he at them. It occurred to him then that whatever they had expected it was not a young man in his shirtsleeves.

"My good man," said the thinner lady, apparently deciding he was a footman, "we have heard that your master is ill. We wished to convey to him our welcome to Ashecombe and our best wishes for his health. Nothing is more efficacious than my calf's-foot jelly or more soothing than Mrs. Elworthy's lavender water."

Nick hardly knew whether to laugh or swear. To be mistaken for a servant twice in a week was proof that he had escaped the rigid ceremonies of Haverly, but it was also a reminder that he, Nick, in himself was nothing. He guessed that these ladies did not even think he had enough consequence to be the butler.

"Thank you, ma'am," he said, and bowed because he thought a footman would. The ladies didn't move. "I'll see that the master gets your gifts straightaway. He cannot receive you, of course."

"Of course," said the ladies together.

"Good day," said Nick, hoping to put an end to the awkward conversation.

He now had a basket in each hand, and he could only close the door with his foot. As that did not seem a proper footmanly act, he backed into the entry, waiting for the ladies to leave. Another awkward moment passed, with the ladies looking at him as if they expected something or someone else.

"Give a hand, then, man," urged the coachman. So Nick put the baskets on the floor and, taking the frailer of the two ladies by the arm, assisted them to their carriage. As he turned to reenter the house, he caught sight of Farre at the stable door, watching the ladies' departure.

In the library, he pulled off his boots and took up the Courtland ledgers again. The ladies' visit puzzled him. He wondered where they had the notion of his being ill. The laconic Farre had certainly not spread any rumors about him in the village. An odd thought came to him that Bel Shaw had said something about him. She would be acquainted with all the country families about Ashecombe. The idea that she had spoken of him, that he had been on her mind, caused a tremor to pass along his body.

He must be a bigger fool than he had ever thought himself to become lost in unprofitable fancies about such a girl. He turned to the accounts of the most prosperous of Courtland's farms, where he might find some profit that would help him restore Courtland. But the gravel of the drive crunched again under the wheels of a vehicle.

After the third caller, he decided to keep his boots on, and after he had closed the door on a fifth, he dropped a basket of lemons beside the other remedies he had received from his new neighbors and turned and strode for the stable.

He found Farre attempting to replace a heavy beam that had once supported a harness rack. Strong as the older man was, he could not hold the beam in place and position the hammer at the same time. Nick stepped up and took the weight of the beam.

"You could have asked for help," he said.

"I could have."

They worked in silence for a few minutes, Farre hammering in the pegs that held the big beam in place, Nick noting all that Farre had accomplished and more that needed to be done. It was time to hire help for his friend. When the task was finished, Farre nodded and began to hang up collars and traces.

"Farre," said Nick, when the older man continued to ignore his presence, "I've been answering my own blasted door all afternoon."

"No ceremony in that, lad."

"Hoist on my own petard. I suppose I deserved it."

Farre paused in the act of coiling a rope. "You could have asked for help."

"I am asking."

"Well then, your lordship, you want me to play the butler?" Farre hung the coiled rope on a peg and turned to Nick. "What do you make of all these visitors?"

"They think I'm ill. That is, they think the earl's ill. They think I'm a footman."

The two men began to stroll toward the house.

"Where do you suppose they got the notion you were ill?"

"I was going to ask you that. Did you say anything in the village about Uncle Miles?" It was possible that someone hearing of his uncle's long illness had confused Nick with his predecessor.

Farre did not answer this but only lifted an eyebrow.

"Oh, I know you didn't. You wouldn't say 'Good day' if it didn't suit you. But five ladies from the village have called to offer fever remedies."

"Ladies, were they?"

"Yes, and don't tell me you didn't look around the corner at every one," said Nick.

"Well then, I suspect a lady told them you were ill."

Nick didn't trust himself to speak. His mind turned that quickly to Bel Shaw.

"Now," said Farre, "why would one lady tell another that a man who can chase a band of poachers off his land single-handed is ill?"

Nick released the breath he was holding. "If Miss Shaw did speak of me to someone, I would not have guessed that she would tell her neighbors I was ill. Ill-mannered, perhaps, but not ill."

"She's not a lass to spare you, is she? Wonder why she said it?"

"You think she meant to send every well-meaning woman in the village to my door?"

Suddenly Farre gave a short bark of laughter. "I'll wager you she did. You said you didn't want her to disturb you again. Well, she found a way around that."

Nick said nothing. He could hear the bubbling laughter of her little band of poachers as it floated to him around a curve of the Ashe. She'd had the last word at their first encounter, and now it seemed she'd scored against him again. Well, he wasn't going to take that without retaliating. But where was he to see her? He doubted she would trespass again, and he could hardly call on her to say what he wanted to say.

Visitors came and went the rest of the afternoon. Nick heard their carriages on the drive and their voices mingling with Farre's. It was late when Farre brought in a tray with the sort of supper the two of them had become accustomed to making. He set it down on the table.

"Thanks," Nick said, though he expected no acknowledgment from his friend. "Seen any likely prospects for our staff?" A sort of grunt was the reply, and Farre disappeared again. He returned a minute later bearing a second tray laden with the baskets and jars they had collected that afternoon.

"What will it be, my lord, Mrs. Pence's posset or Mrs. Nye's calf's-foot jelly? I'm told that both are excellent for the fever," said Farre, bowing with mock seriousness.

Nick reached for a particularly strong-smelling jar, the contents of which appeared to have been gathered from the depths of a murky pond.

"Leeches," said Farre.

"Can I dose Miss Shaw?" Nick asked. Farre looked at him shrewdly then, and Nick returned the jar to the tray. He began to help himself to bread and meat from the first tray.

"You know, lad, your uncle was sick nearly ten years, but no neighbor called or brought him naught. Here you are, a stranger to these folks, and at that girl's word a dozen of your neighbors call with gifts. Odd, don't you think?"

Nick was not fooled by the indifferent tone of this remark. Farre wanted him to consider that. "You think I ought to thank her? I'm not likely to see her again, and if I do, it's not thanking her I had in mind."

"Oh, you can see her. Soon enough, too." It was Farre's turn to serve himself from their tray.

Nick held himself in check while Farre arranged slices of cheese, bread, and cold roast on his plate, while he scooped mustard from the pot and spread it with studied evenness across three slices of bread, while he assembled symmetrical piles of the ingredients.

"Well?" Nick said at last.

"Church, lad—her uncle's the vicar. Go to church." Farre lifted one of the sandwiches he had so carefully composed and bit into it with apparent satisfaction.

6

THE CONGREGATION OF St. Edward's of Ashecombe rose with whispers and a rustle of muslins for the close of the service. Above the stir, the voice of the vicar, Charles Shaw, resounded in rich and solemn tones. "And we thank Thee, Lord, for the timely recovery of the Earl of Haverly."

In the first pew of the little stone church Nick stiffened, conscious of his neighbors' stares at his back. But he was safe. The strangers around him could see only the Earl of Haverly, all that his uncle wanted him to be, while he, Nick, the unwanted offspring of Haverly's wastrel brother, Nick the dreamer and book-reader, was invisible to them under the London coat of gray superfine.

He turned to leave the church, letting his face harden into the aloof lines he had learned from his uncle. Uncle Miles, inches shorter than Nick, had had the knack of looking down his nose as if he were regarding ants from a precipice. If Nick could not rate himself as highly as Uncle Miles had believed an earl should be rated, still Nick had no wish to be mistaken for a servant again. All of Ashecombe was watching, but he looked only for a pair of impertinent blue eyes, found them, and held their gaze. The wariness in those eyes gave him a certain wicked satisfaction.

Outside, he found the vicar waiting to greet him

and was surprised, as he had been in meeting Augustus Shaw, into a kind of intimacy quite unfamiliar to him. Like his brother, Charles Shaw offered a direct gaze, a warm if less forceful handshake, and a question about Courtland that invited Nick to stand among the Shaws in the shade of the elms, explaining what he hoped to achieve at the manor. His gaze strayed toward the door through which Bel Shaw would soon pass, and he wondered what she would think to see him conversing with her parents and uncle.

As soon as Nicholas Seymour passed her in his fine London coat, Bel knew he meant revenge. His glance told her as clearly as words could have that he had seen through the parade of visitors she had sent to his door. But what sort of revenge?

"Did you ever see such a coat?" her cousin Ellen whispered in her ear. She and Ellen had left St. Edward's Church, arms linked, every Sunday of their girlhood, and no one had ever aroused such curiosity in her cousin before. Ellen, nearly eighteen, counted her marriage prospects daily, dreamed fondly of a London season, and believed the cut of a man's coat was a great measure of his worth.

"How old do you think he is, Bel?" came the next whisper.

"Do be quiet, Ellen," Bel urged, frowning at her cousin.

"No one will hear us. Everyone's talking about him anyway." Ellen grinned.

Looking around, Bel saw it was true.

"He can't be older than Darlington, can he?"

"He can be as old as the squire for all it matters to us," said Bel repressively.

"Oh, Bel, he's a single man, of course it matters to us. Besides, he looked right at you. Do you think he's as handsome as Darlington? Do you think his dark straight hair is as fine as Darlington's golden curls? Do you think you could give up Darlington for the earl?"

"Ellen," said Bel as they came out into the churchyard, "the earl will hardly mix with the society of Ashecombe, not in the circles in which the Shaws may move. You shouldn't imagine that his coming here will make the least difference in our lives." *Except to diminish our pleasure in the Ashe.*

Ellen turned her pretty, petulant face to Bel. "But, Bel," she said, "he did come here, even though the season is very much at its height in London. And besides, the Shaws are the best family for miles."

"There are no earls for miles about, and we hardly know what sort of friends Lord Haverly has elsewhere. Did you notice he wears a mourning band? Perhaps he doesn't wish to meet anyone." This remark was apparently lost on Ellen, who had turned her gaze to the crowd in front of them.

"Look," she said, with a defiant toss of her head, "the earl is talking to Uncle Augustus and Uncle Charles now. They'll get him to a Shaw dinner. Sunday sennight—you'll see." Ellen flounced off with a swish of skirts.

Bel slowed her steps. Ellen joined the earl's party, allowing herself to be presented with a pretty blush and curtsy. If Bel joined the group around her parents, would the earl receive her with the same grace? Surely he was gentleman enough to say nothing of their meeting at the river or the dozens of visitors who had come to his door. He looked up, and she halted. The glance he offered her was too challenging by half, as if he dared her to meet him.

The moment she returned his glance, Nick decided Miss Shaw's eyes ought not to be looked at suddenly by the unwary. One minute he was conversing rationally with his new neighbors, the next their words were a faint buzz in his ears, and he had taken a step, had actually taken a step toward Miss Shaw, so that the vicar, who was suggesting the names of reliable craftsmen, was compelled to step back. Nick forced his gaze to return to the man's face, but it was a minute or more before he again caught the meaning of the vicar's words. Bel Shaw was strolling toward them. If he could break away now, he would pass her on the path. His back would be to the others. There was no one behind her. He could say anything he liked for her ears alone.

The earl's gaze had nearly stopped Bel. She saw him step forward and thought fleetingly that he meant to speak after all—there, in front of all the Shaws. Then Alan Darlington stepped in her path.

"Good morning, Bel, looking for me?" His gaze swept over her in a lazy, impertinent perusal.

"Are the Shaws forgiven then . . . Mr. Darlington?" she asked. She had nearly spoken another man's name. She steadied herself.

"They could be, Bel, if you would be kind to me. Come driving this afternoon. Emily Pence and Lyde want to go over to Hilcombe, and Mrs. Pence will allow it, if you come along."

She weighed the idea. Emily was waving from John Lyde's curricle across the road. To say yes would be a kindness to her friend, but Darlington's friendly offer coming so soon after he had vowed revenge against her made her wary. She could not think properly. Somewhere behind the breadth of Darlington's shoulders was the earl with his dark, piercing glance. She had seen him take a step toward her. Was he watching at this moment?

"Your parents would like you to favor my suit, Bel," said Darlington, "and you know you should. You will in the end anyway."

She forgot the earl in a surge of irritation with

Darlington. When had he begun to think that the friendship of their two families made a marriage between the two of them as inevitable as next Sunday's sermon?

She answered in her coolest tone. "I will go driving with you, Mr. Darlington, thank you, but anything more I cannot promise."

He shrugged. "We'll see. Two?"

She nodded, and he bowed and strolled off.

The earl was standing quite close really, preparing to mount his horse. He regarded her briefly with that gaze of his, and she looked away at once. Had he overheard her conversation with Darlington? She looked again in his direction, but he was riding off. Would he think she had meant something by looking at him so? How silly she was about the Earl of Haverly. She had best put him out of her mind.

At two Farre found Nick's horse back in his stall as neat as could be. All that a groom might teach a peer Farre had taught Nick, but in this matter of love, the groom's hands were tied. And in this matter, Farre suspected, his lordship was still something of a boy in spite of all that the boy had seen in the odd household of his parents.

Today Farre had been caught napping, for he meant to keep a sharp eye out for every promising sign of the lad's interest in their neighbor. The girl with the blue, blue eyes and golden curls seemed to have caught his lordship fairly, and Farre could not let the boy go it alone. Nick would be at the river, and Farre would just wander down to see what had come of his lordship's fine dreams of revenge.

"So you went," said Farre. Nick was standing on a rock overhanging the first of the deep, well-shaded pools that distinguished Courtland's stretch of the Ashe. "Did you see Miss Shaw?"

"Yes." Nick did not look up, but made a show of watching the drift of his line in the current.

"Speak to her?" Farre had the satisfaction of seeing his lordship jerk the line in a manner unlikely to deceive the least canny trout.

"No. She had an admirer."

"A golden-haired fellow with shoulders you could hitch a plow to?"

"How did you know that?" Nick was frowning at the water. He lifted the lure from the stream with a deft flick of his wrist and pulled in to prepare another cast.

"Squire's boy. Met him when I spoke to the agent about this property. Stands to reason he'd be after the prettiest girl about."

"So you think she's the prettiest girl about?"

The studied indifference of the question gave Farre a good bit of encouragement. "A great bull like the squire's boy, his importance won't let him notice anyone but the prettiest."

Nick made a clumsy cast, allowing fly and line to slap the water. He swore and withdrew his line again. "The fellow is welcome to Miss Rag Manners, of course," he said, bringing his arm back for another try.

"You think she wants him?" asked Farre.

At that Nick turned, and the smooth curve of his line, instead of floating gently down to the glassy surface of the pool, caught on a branch. "If you want supper tonight, Farre," he warned, "you had best be gone and let me forget Miss Shaw."

"If you think you can, lad." Farre found himself whistling a bit as he went up the path, an old tune, one that hadn't come to mind since . . . since Nan was alive.

7

AT TWO BEL found Darlington in her mother's rose drawing room talking with Auggie. Her visitor half-lay, half-sat on a silk sofa with his long legs stretched out as if he were at home before his own fire. When he saw Bel, he stood and strolled her way.

"I was just offering your brothers a chance to fish our end of the Ashe," he said.

"How kind," said Bel, looking at Auggie, unable to conceal her surprise.

"Well, it *is* pretty sporting," said Auggie, not quite meeting his sister's gaze. He bent over and gave the retriever at his feet a gratuitous rub.

"Of course," she said. Auggie's expression was decidedly sheepish and unlike him.

"Now, Bel," said Darlington, "is this coolness to be my only reward for trying to make amends?"

"Thank you, Mr. Darlington," she said. "It is kind of you to think of my brothers. Your father has no objection to their fishing his waters?" The Darlingtons had never before been so generous with their stretch of the river.

"None."

"Hurrah!" shouted Auggie. He dashed off with what seemed to Bel an uncharacteristically craven air, the dog barking excitedly at his heels.

"Shall we, Bel?" Darlington asked, offering his arm to escort her. She nodded. He seemed too pleased with himself for her comfort, as if he'd won some victory over her.

In the drive, her father's coachman held the heads of Darlington's team, a pair of grays that Tom had always admired. Emily Pence and John Lyde, newly betrothed, called greetings from a second carriage. Bel chided herself at the sight of them. Perhaps Darlington's intentions were kind after all, and she merely cynical. Surely the friendship of their families mattered as much to him as it did to her, and if he sometimes lost his temper and made threats, weren't they just threats, such as her brothers made to one another?

Darlington didn't speak again until they passed her father's gates and turned onto the open road. Then he began to question her about Tom's ship and situation. The gradually rising road gave them wide prospects of the valley below.

Just as Bel began to feel ashamed that she had unjustly suspected some trick in Darlington's kindnesses to herself and her brothers, Darlington turned his team aside and stopped the phaeton at the brow of the hill. He pointed to the sparkle of the Ashe far below them. They were alone. Somehow, without her noticing it, their betrothed companions had fallen behind. Bel glanced along the road they had come, but there was no sign of the other carriage.

"Now, Bel, we can come to an understanding," he said.

"Mr. Darlington, we *have* an understanding. Our parents are friends, you and my brothers are friends, I would remain your friend."

"You are too proud, Bel. All you Shaws. You think you still have acres and acres behind you and a fair dowry." He laughed. "Or is it Haverly? I wonder, does his fortune tempt you? Did you mean to gain an advantage over all the other fair damsels of

Ashecombe by poaching his stream and gaining his notice first?"

Bel stiffened. Auggie must have told him of their encounter with the earl. "What advantage could I have or want?" she asked as coolly as she could. "What do you mean bringing me here and having the effrontery to speak so?"

"I'll speak any way I want to. You owe me. An earl is not for you. Pretty as you are, a hundred a year is all you will have from your proud papa." He paused and turned to her, letting his gaze slide over her. "Even for me that's low."

"You needn't lower yourself, Mr. Darlington. I have never encouraged you to think of me in any way."

"But you have, Bel, you do. How could I not want the prettiest girl in Ashecombe? How could I not win the prize now when I've come so close?" His voice was soft, his hands careless on the reins, his assurance the most maddening thing of all.

"I'm not a prize to be won, and you may court whom you please."

"It pleases me to court you, and you know it is what the Shaws expect. What Tom expects. You can't do better, and you must do something for Diana so she can have a come-out and Arthur so he can go to Oxford." Darlington set the brake and secured the reins to it.

"Mr. Darlington . . ."

"Alan," he said, "or *darling*. You didn't call me *Mister* when you were fourteen, Bel. Didn't you dream of my kisses that summer you followed Tom and me everywhere?"

"No."

"That's a lie, Bel. You kissed Lyde."

"Years ago."

"And that fellow from Ireland, that friend of Tom's. You're kissable, Bel, but I'll wager you've not been properly kissed yet." He reached out and caught her hand. She pulled away, but he stopped her, pinning her arms behind her and securing a hold on her with one hand.

"Let me go," she demanded.

"No." He pulled her close on the narrow seat and brushed the folds of her pelisse back over her shoulder, exposing the neckline of her dress. Bel squirmed, fighting his hold. She looked toward the road, hoping to see the others. The horses stirred restlessly in response to the jiggling of the carriage, but Darlington spoke reassurances to them. He turned back to Bel, and with the forefinger of his free hand he traced the edge of her bodice, letting the weight of that finger pull the delicate muslin lower than the modest height at which she wore it.

Bel glared at him defiantly, refusing to be intimidated by his tactics. "If I ever wanted you to kiss me, *Mr.* Darlington . . ." He squeezed her wrists painfully, and she went on, ". . . it was because I thought you were like my brother, kind and honorable. But I see you are not."

"Oh, I'm like your precious Tom, all right. I can tell you things about your dear brother, Bel, but let's not quarrel." The words slowed, and his voice thickened. He pulled her so close that they were pressed together, hip to knee. "I just want a kiss. You'll like it, Bel. Girls do."

Darlington slid his free hand up her arm along the bare skin between her wrist and shoulder, slowly lowering his face to hers. Bel struggled helplessly, her mind considering and rejecting means of escape. She felt his breath hot against her skin and redoubled her efforts, tossing her head from side to side. Darlington caught the ribands of her bonnet and yanked hard. Her hat fell back, and he caught her chin in his hand.

"Give it up, sweetheart," he said. "I've caught you fairly this time, and there's no Auggie to save you."

The mention of Auggie put an idea in Bel's mind, and she stopped fighting Darlington's hold on her chin as if resigned to his assault. He leaned forward, his fingers loosening to stroke her skin. She waited motionless as he drew near, slowly filling her lungs, afraid lest he suspect her intention. Just as his lips were to touch hers, she turned her head slightly and gave the loudest, most piercing whistle her brothers had ever taught her.

Darlington started back, cursing and clutching the ear that had borne the brunt of her attack. The horses reared and backed against the carriage, rocking it dangerously. Darlington released Bel to control his team, and Bel, her hands freed, twisted away from him and leapt down from the phaeton. The landing jarred her feet in her thin slippers, but she didn't flinch. She righted her bonnet, retied the strings, and pulled her pelisse about her shoulders. With these repairs to her person accomplished, she faced her brother's friend.

"Mr. Darlington, neither your friendship with my brother, nor your parents' friendship with mine, obliges me to endure your conceit or your attentions any longer. I do not and will not favor your suit." She turned and slipped into the woods.

"A fine speech, Bel," Darlington called after her. "But it doesn't end what's between us."

8

≪≪≪≪≪≪≪≪≪≪≪

Nick stared at the surface of the pool that had in a fortnight become his favorite. It was the largest and deepest of three shady pools that descended like a short flight of sleek, black steps from the hill on which Courtland Manor had been built to the meadows below. This morning, however, hunks of bread, thickly strewn, lay on the water as if there had been a bread blizzard in the night. While peppering the waters of a stream with bread was an old practice that even Walton recommended, someone had gone far beyond that angler's technique. As Nick watched, a trout rose lazily, nibbled with unhurried delicacy at the soggy mass, and slipped back into the depths.

Nick swore.

"Not likely manna from heaven, is it?" said Farre at Nick's side.

"Rather malice from a much more local source." Nick stepped forward, but Farre's hand on his arm stayed him.

"Let's have a close look at the ground here, lad," said Farre, pointing at several boot prints visible in the mud. He put his own boot alongside one of the clearest prints as a measurement. The intruder had worn a small but decidedly masculine boot.

A thorough examination of the edge of the pool revealed more of the same boot prints and dozens of dog prints.

"Whoever your visitor was," Farre speculated, "he isn't a hungry fellow. He needs neither bread, nor trout. Spent good money, too. Fine white bread."

"Boys, a dog, no hunger, and enough knowledge of the Ashe to spoil the best pool. I can guess who the trespassers were," said Nick.

"Perhaps," said Farre. "But you might want a bit more evidence yet."

Evidence proved easy to come by. Two days later someone attempted to dam a portion of the stream above the pools and left a distinct shred of wool breeches on the end of a sharp branch. Twice Nick had the satisfaction of scaring the trespassers off, if not the satisfaction of apprehending them. Then, the day they succeeded in damming one of the pools with a large boulder, he found the green cap. He knew he'd seen it before on one of the Shaws.

Farre, currying a promising mare, only grunted when Nick showed him the incriminating article.

"Well, it's the proof I need, isn't it?" Nick asked.

"So," came the reply, "are you going to take your accusations to her father?" Farre's head came up, and his gaze met Nick's squarely.

Ay, there's the rub, Nick thought.

He could not see white morning light on the surface of the Ashe without recalling Bel Shaw. The jars and baskets his neighbors had brought lined a shelf in the great bare kitchen of the manor, reminding him of Bel. And the girl whose gaze had caused him such confusion outside the little stone church invaded his dreams nightly. It was a mere two days till the Shaws' dinner. He returned to his library and dropped the cap on his desk. He could afford to be patient for two days.

The next morning brought the men and materials to restore the stable, and directing their work drove all thoughts of the trespasser from Nick's mind. He was beginning to understand his uncle's obsession with Haverly, with making something fine and enduring and *his*. He did not think of the attacks on his stream again until he came awake in the dark, his senses aroused by some subtle difference in the feel of the night around him. With his next breath Nick knew what it was. The waterwheel had stopped, and somewhere outside his room a fire was burning.

When he reached the burning timbers, timbers that only that afternoon had been numbered and stacked, he knew his project had been sabotaged, but he didn't stop to blink. He found Farre ordering the master carpenter's men into a bucket chain from the cistern to the blaze. A quick inspection showed that in spite of the stopped wheel, the cistern held enough water to put out the fire, so Nick joined the line. He passed bucket after bucket along the line of quick hands, his anger as palpable a heat in him as the fire that reddened his face and brought sweat to his brow.

With the dawn Nick and Farre and the master carpenter inspected the waterwheel and found the severed pulley that had rendered the machine useless. The carpenter took an optimistic view of the damage, assuring Nick that both the wheel and the stable roof could be restored by his workers. But Nick hardly listened. The odor of charred timbers was in his nostrils; Farre's face, weary and soot-smeared, was before him; and the prints of certain boots and paws were clear in the mud. His mind rapidly calculated the earliest moment when he could lodge his complaint with Mr. Augustus Shaw.

From the morning room Bel saw the earl approach the door of Shaw House. The haste of his dismount, the urgency of his stride, and the implacable expression on his handsome face told her he was not merely making a neighborly call. The bell rang with a note of jangling insistence she had not imagined such a mechanism could convey. Then Jenner knocked discreetly on the morning-room door.

"Miss Bel, Lord Haverly to see your father."

"Thank you, Jenner," she said, rising slowly. A little curl of steam drifted up from her teacup, and she regarded it wistfully. She wished her parents were home. Once again her father had gone to Hilcombe on behalf of the accused villagers, and this time her mother had accompanied him. Bel shook out her skirts. Jenner was holding the door for her.

"Dick and I will be about, Miss, should you need us," Jenner whispered as Bel passed.

Darkly clad, his back to her, Haverly stood looking out the tall windows at the far end of the rose drawing room. He did not appear to have heard her enter. His left hand hung clenched at his side, and his right slapped his gloves against his thigh impatiently.

She had imagined her next meeting with him would be at her uncle's dinner, surrounded by all the Shaws. There she meant to be cordial and indifferent, giving the earl no more than civil smiles and exchanging no challenging glances with him. With his sudden arrival at her door, she was embarrassed to have given any thought to the matter of seeing him at all. She did not know how to begin with him. He seemed so threatening in the soft sunny room with its chintzes, its vases of roses, its dusting of pollen on the polished tables.

"Good morning, Lord Haverly," she said. He whirled to face her, and she had the satisfaction of observing surprise and consternation in his dark eyes. Apparently she had thrown him off balance.

Nick recovered and turned away immediately. Had the man misunderstood his request? He could not see Bel Shaw just now. Seeing her so close would make him mush-brained, and the arguments he meant to make must remain clear in his mind. "I came to see your father," he said, "in his capacity as magistrate."

This bit of rudeness did little for Bel's resolve to play the gracious hostess in her parents' absence; nevertheless, she invited her visitor to sit, informing him that her parents were in Hilcombe for the morning.

"If you wish to relate your business to me, Lord Haverly, I will tell my father of it as soon as he returns," she offered, seating herself on a pale blue sofa opposite the window where the earl stood. He stared at her for a minute but made no move to sit in any of the chairs near her.

Relate his business to her? In a room full of the unbearable softness of roses while she herself looked as delicate as petals against the sky. "*Will* you tell your father the reason for my call? I wonder, Miss Shaw. You may not wish to give my complaint to your father when you hear what it is."

"Lord Haverly, I am not in the habit of withholding messages from my father." The man meant to insult her again, and she was forced to remind herself that the earl had a claim to her father's justice and she must act calmly and justly in her father's place. She folded her hands in her lap and looked up at him with as civil an expression as she could manage. She would not offer Lord Haverly any refreshment.

"Very well," said the earl. He stood opposite her, his back to the windows now. "Tell your father I have been troubled since Sunday last with attacks upon my stretch of the Ashe, with persons who have polluted the stream, and dammed it twice." His gaze challenged her.

"I will."

"Tell him I suspect your brothers."

"No!" She jumped up and strode toward him, stopping just inches from where he stood. "My brothers have not been near your stretch of the Ashe since the day we met," she said, giving to each word a distinctness and emphasis that could hardly be mistaken.

He did not move or look away, but met her anger with an unflinching gaze of his own. "How can you be sure of that?" he asked.

Now she saw what folly she'd been guilty of in giving in to Auggie and her cousins that day. She had brought them all under suspicion. "My brothers are neither criminals nor sneaks. When we fished the Lower Ashe in the past, we did so openly, with the permission granted to the trustee. Your purchasing Courtland put an end to our fishing there."

"Yet you were fishing there the day I arrived. And that was poaching, was it not? Would not your brothers, resentful of my claim to the Ashe and encouraged by your own example, take vengeance on me if they saw the chance?"

"My example encourage criminal acts?" They had come to her next folly. In his eyes she saw his awareness of her petty revenge against him. Suddenly she felt small and childish next to him. The comfortable muslin she had chosen for a Saturday at home seemed absurdly girlish, her dignity impossible to maintain. Her hands shook, but she concealed their shaking in the folds of her gown. She was Augustus Shaw's daughter. Her brothers were not furtive, desperate characters with no respect for the law, and this earl could not insult them so. Did he in his pride imagine that the Shaws had none? He was unbearable. He deserved no justice from her. "I will tell my father you have a complaint to make, Lord Haverly."

She meant to dismiss him, he saw. It was time to nod and bow and withdraw, but though his mind understood her intent, his body would not obey. She was too near, and a taut weakness held him rooted to the spot. The morning sun streaming through the tall windows burnished her hair and the tips of her lashes, and her eyes burned blue. "It is not only attacks on the river, but wanton destruction as well. Last night someone severed the main pulley on my waterwheel and set fire to the timbers which were to restore my stable."

She gasped. He accused her brothers of no less a crime than the one of the poor villagers her father meant to defend. "You imagine my brothers were in any way responsible for such acts?"

He had provoked her defiance now. It was there in the deceptive sweetness of her voice. "I have evidence," he said.

"Evidence against boys who lay asleep in their beds while someone else set fire to your lumber and damaged your waterwheel? Acts which boys could hardly have done?"

She seemed now to imply that he was absurd, and her tone roused him from the lethargy that her nearness had created. His anger was back, and he felt powerless to contain it. For the first time in his life he had something that was wholly his, not Haverly's, not something carelessly abandoned by his parents, but his, and he would not endure any trespass against it. "Should I not accuse the only poachers I have caught in the act? Should I not suspect that those who would poach boldly by daylight would do worse under the concealment of night? Should I not suspect boys led by an unprincipled young woman, boys whose father knew my plans for Courtland better than any?"

"You accuse me of lack of principle? My father of indifference to his children's honor?"

"I do." They were glaring at each other now, and he was conscious of a desire to force her to drop her gaze from his.

"And this is the message you wish me to convey to my father upon his return?"

She was daring him, pushing him to say it, and he would. "It is."

For an instant she looked stunned. Then her eyes became cold. "Lord Haverly, as my father is the most principled and fair of men, he will want to know of these crimes against your property. I will tell him the facts as you have conveyed them to me. I will not, however, mention your accusations against the Shaws. Those you must make when you meet him."

She did not openly dare him, but the proud lift of her chin and the steadiness of her gaze told him he was being dared all the same. "I will," he said.

"Then, Lord Haverly, know this," she said. "I will never forgive you for your insults to my family. Good day." She gave him a curt nod and was gone before he had time to think himself a very great fool.

Saturday evening

Dear Tom,

You must know that everyone here has you in mind and wishes for your safety and prosperity. If it is foolish to wish for both, then you must allow us to be foolish on your behalf, for though you must encounter danger if you are to prosper, I hope it is very little danger compared with the greatness of the prizes you take.

Without word from you I cannot be sure which of my letters has reached you and must begin at the beginning of my news. We are troubled with a new neighbor, the Earl of Haverly. His purchase of Courtland Manor and lands has ended Father's trusteeship of that property and our pleasure in the Ashe. I am sure it need not be so except that the earl is a cold, arrogant, possessive man. His pride is unbearable, and I cannot begin to tell you the half of his insults to the Shaws. You would feel obliged to call him out

and that would not do. You must concern yourself with the Turks, and I must fight this battle
on my own. I am not without resources against
such an enemy, and when you are home again,
Tom, I will tell you of a small victory against the
earl.

Of course, everyone toad-eats him but the
Shaws, and he has taken us in dislike and ac-
cuses *us* of attacks on *his* stream and property.
He made such accusations to me as you will
hardly credit, suggesting that our brothers have
been responsible for damming his stream and
setting fire to timber on his property.

Father and Mother cannot see his arrogance.
They see only the London air and fine coats. Indeed, Father takes the man altogether too seriously. If the earl summons, Father goes, like the
veriest lackey in the man's hire. It is as if in purchasing Courtland, his lordship had purchased
us all. Today, Father returned from hours of
work in Hilcombe and rode immediately to hear
the earl's latest complaint. And what is worse,
Uncle Charles has invited the man to a Shaw
dinner tomorrow night. Well, after what he has
said to me today, I can hardly be civil to him no
matter whose drawing room he enters, but I suppose it is rather unlikely that his lordship will
deign to sit down to one of Aunt Margaret's dinners. It is too bad, really, for her custard might
melt his arrogant heart.

No doubt you will hear more favorable accounts of our new neighbor from others, but you
may trust me not to be blinded by the man's
coats and the rumors of his vast acres.

Your loving sister,
Isabel

9

THE RESULT OF gathering so large a family as the Shaws into so modest a room as the vicarage parlor was an unsettled scene, like the crowding of spectators at a mill or an auction. Yet from the threshold Nick was able to distinguish Bel Shaw among all her fair-haired relations. She was sitting on a faded green velvet chair, her golden head bent toward a small boy, who cupped some treasure in his outstretched hands, offering it to her. She might have been Titania on a moss-covered stump in the forest, so regal and solemn was her air, so delicate the gown that flowed over her knees.

As Nick was announced, she looked up, glanced coldly at him, and returned her gaze to the boy. Nick had a fleeting recollection of himself as a boy venturing into the drawing room during one of his parents' house parties and retreating at such a glance from his mother. The Earl of Haverly need not retreat, however, and he stepped forward. His host and hostess claimed his attention, leading him toward a red-haired gentleman of imposing dimensions, made grander by the brilliance of a yellow waistcoat. Beside him was a tall woman in white with an immobility of countenance that made her appear as if she were carved in stone. As Nick guessed, these were the Darlingtons.

Then the younger Darlington was presented to Nick.

Their eyes met, and Nick knew that his dislike of the man was reciprocated. Darlington's shoulders were every bit as broad as Nick remembered, the man's hands large and heavy, the face, handsome, Nick supposed. Women must admire such a face, with its smooth, regular features and cool green eyes.

"A pretty stretch of the Ashe you purchased, Haverly," said Darlington. "Are you an angler?"

"I've been known to flog a stream," said Nick.

"You'll be lucky to keep the Ashe to yourself then. The Shaws have fished that stretch forever."

Was there a deliberate challenge in the words, or did Nick imagine the mockery in them? "So I've been told," he replied.

"Lord Haverly," interrupted his host, "let me present my other brother." In the next half hour Nick encountered such a bewildering number of fair-haired, blue-eyed people named Shaw that he had to exert himself steadily to remember who was who. Twice he encountered members of the fishing party he had chased off his property. When presented, they responded like well-schooled children, but their eyes did not meet his, and their unease renewed the suspicions Nick meant to lay to rest. He was considering the sullen look of Auggie Shaw when dinner was announced.

Mrs. Charles Shaw, the vicar's wife, appeared startled for a moment, as if she had had no notion that they were all dining at her table. Then she called to the children, shooing them toward a maid servant at the door.

"Dear," she addressed her husband, "you must lead us." The Shaws began to move toward the door with a sort of confusion Nick had never witnessed in his uncle's house. In the stir he found himself face-to-face with Bel Shaw.

"Oh dear," Mrs. Charles Shaw said, "I never presented you to my niece, did I, Lord Haverly? Miss

Shaw, Lord Haverly." They were surrounded by all her relatives, but, in that moment of bustle and change, all fell silent, or perhaps Nick simply no longer heard them. What Bel might have done had the introduction been made more discreetly, he could not guess. But under these circumstances, he knew she would have to acknowledge him.

"Miss Shaw," he said, inclining his head with a slight bow and extending his hand. She would have to take it, and he would touch her though she wished him a hundred miles away.

"My lord," she said. Her eyes flashed defiance, but after a hesitation so slight he felt only he had noticed it, her hand met his. An act of will was required to allow him to let her go. In her action there was every appearance of appropriate reserve between strangers, but he felt his face must show how stirred he had been at the brief touch. He did not know how he came to be seated in the dining room with Mrs. Darlington on his right and his hostess on his left. Soup had been served, and his hostess regarded him expectantly. He smiled and raised his spoon.

Bel did not know where to look. Her hand tingled from the brief touch of the earl's. She had turned from him to find her mother's gaze on her, not unkind but cautioning. Clearly, her mother had recognized the unease of Bel's meeting with the earl and wondered at it. Darlington, too, had seen her encounter with Haverly. Now, to her left across the table, he glared at her.

The earl was at the far end of the table between Mrs. Darlington and Aunt Margaret, and Bel's wayward gaze sought his without her will. To her dismay, every glance of her own down the length of the crowded table seemed to be detected by her mother or Darlington.

The earl's silence seemed to reproach her family's

hearty volubility. Familiar anecdotes that had amused Bel, no matter how frequently repeated, now seemed self-absorbed and vain. Even Augustus Shaw seemed to have too much to say. Uncle Fletcher proposed a toast to the earl's health. Ellen stared at the man with a steadiness that would have done credit to a cat. Then Aunt Margaret served poached trout, to which Darlington called everyone's attention with a fulsome compliment that set Aunt Margaret to apologizing.

"Oh, dear, my lord, you must wonder what I was thinking. But trout are so lovely poached . . . in wine, of course, with tarragon and basil."

Again Bel could not help but look his way. Again he seemed to anticipate her glance and meet it. Her aunt was explaining the poaching process in detail, elaborating on the mix of herbs and wine, and blushing more with every mention of *poach* or *poached* or *poaching*. For a minute Bel thought his solemn eyes brightened with mirth. Then her father came to her aunt's rescue with an account of Uncle Charles' fishing for the trout in question right behind the vicarage.

By then Bel had no notion of what she was eating or what was being said around her. Threads of conversation from his end of the table tangled in her mind with the remarks of those around her so that she didn't dare reply to Phil, her dinner partner. Really, she was behaving foolishly, and Phil did not deserve such inattention from her. He was but newly promoted to Aunt Margaret's company table and doing his best. He furrowed his handsome brow, adjusted the unfamiliar cravat at his throat, and plunged on with his subject. Her eldest brother, Richard, on her left, expected no more from her than a nod of agreement from time to time. This she could comfortably give as Richard, in spite of heroic action at Talavera and Badajos, never said anything which could not be consented to by the entire population of the nation.

Bel welcomed the arrival of Aunt Margaret's custard and the suggestion that soon followed that the ladies should adjourn, but Bel's father rose as well.

"Charles, the ladies have the advantage if we let them depart now. I say we all step out into your garden. The evening's as fine a one as we're likely to have this summer."

"My lord? Squire?" asked Charles Shaw, looking to the earl and Squire Darlington.

At the earl's agreement, chairs were pushed back, linens dropped, voices raised. A servant came forward to open the double doors at the end of the room, and the guests moved out onto a low stone terrace and from it to the lawn that stretched to the river below.

Bel held back a little, resolving to take herself firmly in hand. How had the presence of one new person so altered her behavior at a family dinner— the same sort of dinner she had reported in detail to Tom not weeks earlier? Tonight she was sure she remembered nothing except the earl's eyes. What could she write her brother? *Dined with the Earl of Haverly. His eyes are as dark as pools of night. His gaze makes me hot in the coolest muslin.*

She had not been herself since the earl had come to Ashecombe. She felt oddly restless and in need of something, some adventure, some chance to act, to take some part in larger affairs, as Tom was doing. That, she supposed, was what Tom had been feeling that summer he had tried to kiss every girl in the county. He probably no longer thought about kissing at all, not while the Turks attacked British ships. If only she had Turks to battle, she would not be staring at the empty custard cups, thinking about . . . *kissing*.

When Bel stepped out on the terrace, the Shaws

had drifted down across the sloping lawn toward the river, which took a lazy turn here behind the vicarage. Her mother and the other women were strolling in the rose garden. Her father and uncles were leading the earl and the squire closer to the river, where Auggie and Joe were punting. Ellen hovered between the group with the earl, and Darlington, who lagged behind them. From the left where the river lay hidden behind a stand of willows came her niece and nephew, Kit and Sarah, running and calling her name. Diana followed her young charges. Bel turned and crossed the lawn to meet them.

"Auntie Bel, come see what we found," urged Sarah, easily outdistancing her younger brother.

"What is it?" asked Bel.

"Frogs," said Kit, "new ones. Just this big." He put his chubby forefingers together so there was no space between them. His stockings were wet and mud-streaked and limp about his ankles, and there were bits of sedge tangled about his shoes.

"And you can catch them right in your hands," said Sarah. Her skirts bore prints of wet hands.

"Do you have a pail to put them in?" asked Bel.

"Yes, come see, come see, Auntie Bel," said Kit.

"Well, of course," said Bel, allowing herself to be tugged along by her impatient nephew. "Clever girl," she said to Diana as they reached her.

"Do you think so, Bel? Won't Aunt be livid that I've let them spoil their clothes?"

"She will hardly notice, when you've kept them so happily busy. Do you want to go on? I'll go with them to the frogs."

"Thanks, Bel," said Diana, and turned to the crowd watching the older boys punt.

Nick watched Bel Shaw pass the other women and come down the lawn toward two small children. "Auntie Bel" he heard them call, and saw Bel stoop to listen to whatever they had to say. The three disappeared along a path at the river's edge. If he could follow without his absence being remarked, he might talk to Miss Shaw and win some good opinion from her.

He knew from his meeting with her father the afternoon before that he had been hasty in his judgment of her family. His complaints had nearly choked him in her mother's drawing room he had been so angry, had felt so taken in. But he had returned to Courtland to find the waterwheel already repaired and the work on the stable underway as if nothing untoward had happened. Then Augustus Shaw had appeared. He had patiently examined the damaged timbers and pulley, questioned all the carpenter's men, the master carpenter, Farre, and Nick. The man's thoroughness, his energy and attention, spoke an integrity Nick could not doubt. He did not present the incriminating cap. In light of Mr. Shaw's actions, Nick's anger, vented on a lovely young woman, had seemed a boorish thing. He had had to come tonight, if only to apologize to Miss Shaw.

He turned back to the punting race and found himself obliged to talk to, or rather to listen to, Miss Fletcher, who had appeared at his side. The next time he glanced down the river, he saw Darlington disappear along the path Bel had taken. The other man's manner reminded him of his own lustful thoughts about Miss Shaw, and he considered how to free himself from the company. Just then the punters called for new passengers, and Miss Fletcher and Phillip Shaw pressed forward toward a short dock to join the others. Nick strode purposefully away.

The party on the bank was calling encouragement to the boys in the boats as he reached the turn where the path led through the willows. He hesitated there, considering how foolish he would feel if he came upon Bel Shaw and Darlington in a lovers' embrace, but the recollection of Darlington's predatory look spurred him on.

He had gone but a few steps more when the two children came stumbling along the path, struggling with a pail. They halted abruptly, sloshing water and frogs onto the ground, and looked at him doubtfully, as if they expected some reproof. He realized he was frowning and, softening his look, reached down to retrieve an escaping frog.

"Here," he said, dropping the tiny creature into the pail. "Don't hurry now, or you'll spill them."

Solemn and still, they nodded at him.

"Go on," he said, stepping aside, and they did, obviously relieved to escape him. He followed the path around another bend of the river and heard angry voices above the smooth slipping of the water.

"How dare you, here where you are a guest of the Shaws," he heard Bel say.

"No one will blame me. I've told you before, Bel, our families expect us to make a match. Unless your mother has designs on the earl."

"No one in my family has designs on the earl, and if you are being so unpleasant because you think me enamored of him, you couldn't be more wrong. I never wish to speak to the man again."

"Again, Bel? How often have you seen him since you poached his river?"

"Auggie told you, didn't he?"

"Told me a good bit, but there are things Auggie's too young to see."

"Well, there aren't things that Auggie's too young to see between me and the Earl of Haverly, and whatever I've said to him, I have nothing to say to you, so let me pass."

"Oh, no, Bel, it's time you learned what kissing is and stopped thinking you're different from other girls."

"Darlington, let me go."

At that plea, uttered with sharp urgency, Nick stepped around the curve. Bel and her assailant faced each other where the path had bulged to make a small clearing. Darlington, his feet planted wide, held the struggling Bel about the waist and was attempting to capture her hands while she writhed in his grasp and pummeled his chest with her fists. Her lovely white dress was twisted about her waist and pulled up above her ankles, and Nick was surprised at the strength of his desire to hit Darlington.

"The lady apparently doesn't wish for your attentions, Mr. Darlington," he said, keeping his voice as level and pleasant as he could.

The man whirled, releasing Bel, who stumbled back against the willow branches. Nick looked once at her eyes, which were wide with surprise, anger, and injured pride, and he turned to face Darlington.

"You know her wishes, Haverly?"

"I could not help but overhear her express them quite plainly just now."

"You followed us." Darlington took a belligerent step toward Nick.

"I merely came along the path as anyone might do."

"Well, you'd best turn back and let old friends settle their differences privately."

"I think not," said Nick. The phrase "old friends" might have stopped him but for the look he caught in Bel Shaw's eyes. Darlington's gaze followed his.

"She's been kissed before, Haverly, so you needn't fear for her maidenly sensibilities. She invites it, you know."

"If she invites you to stay, Darlington, I will leave."

"Well, Bel?" Darlington addressed this remark over his shoulder.

"Please go, Mr. Darlington" was the reply. Bel had

made no attempt to repair the disorder of her dress, yet she seemed no less the fairy queen.

Darlington turned as if he could not believe what he was hearing. "You can't afford to let me go, Bel," he said.

"Nevertheless, Mr. Darlington, please go." She spoke proudly, her chin lifted, her gaze unyielding.

"You owe me, Bel, and you'll pay. Remember that."

Bel held herself steady. Darlington's threats must be taken seriously, she knew, and she feared that he would turn his resentment against one of her brothers. Gentle Arthur had been Darlington's target before, but even Auggie was not safe from Darlington in one of his savage moods. Still he must see she would not bend on this. Then he laughed.

"At least I mean marriage, Bel. With your hundred pounds a year, you can hardly ask that of Haverly."

Abruptly he turned and strode toward the earl, who stepped aside neatly to let his adversary pass. Darlington could be heard swearing and breaking branches until he passed beyond a curve in the path. Then Bel looked up to find the earl's dark eyes on her. Of all people, to be humiliated before him. Nothing could be more awkward. She was suddenly conscious of the disorder of her person. She could feel wisps of hair about her face, and his gaze made her white gown feel as insubstantial as mist.

When their eyes met, he seemed to recall himself and looked away. "I don't doubt you are surprised by my intervention," he began. "I had no right, but I hope you will accept it as well meant."

Her sense of justice demanded that she thank him, but it was difficult to say the words. "Thank you," she said at last.

"Will you take my arm?" he offered. "I'll walk you back to your family."

He was looking at her again with that unsettling intensity. "No . . . that is, you must excuse me. I must . . ." She reached up to catch a curl at her neck. ". . . do something with my hair and gown."

"I can wait," he said.

"No," she protested. She could not regain her composure if he stood there looking at her as he was. "You needn't wait. I know how heartily you disapprove of me."

At that a different expression crossed his face, almost of embarrassment, she thought, and he looked away toward the river.

"You hardly know how I think of you at all," he said, his voice low. "I have been rude. Let me be civil this once."

"Why?"

"I want your good opinion," he said.

"And you think a moment's accidental gallantry can win it after what you have said about the Shaws—about me?" She didn't know why she was belittling his kindness except that he looked at her in a way that recalled all her foolishness at dinner and her thoughts of kissing and her embarrassment at every encounter between them.

"Accidental? You think me incapable of courtesy? I suppose you might. Having met your brothers and seen such gallantry as you are accustomed to from your suitors, I see you can have no notion of how a gentleman might behave. But your ignorance of gentlemanly behavior does not excuse me from the exercise of it. So I will wait, and I will escort you back to your family."

"Gentlemanly behavior," she scoffed. "Your courtesies are no better than Darlington's advances if you force them on me."

"Think what you will, but until someone comes along the path to rescue you from my excesses of civility, you are as trapped with me as you were with him." Somehow during this exchange the earl had closed the distance between them, and Bel could see a dangerous glint of resolve in his eyes. He paused. "Now," he said, "I'll turn my back if you wish to straighten your hair and gown."

He did so, blocking the path so that she could neither pass him through the tangle of willow branches nor step around him through the mud and reeds at the river's edge. She stared at his elegant back in the gray coat. How could she have thought him at all shepherd-like? The man had not an ounce of humility in his whole person.

She smoothed her gown and hair as quickly as she could.

"I'm ready," she said. He turned, and she refused to look at him but took the arm he offered. Once or twice as they walked along, she felt him looking at her and thought that he might speak, but she kept her face resolutely turned from his. When the path brought them back to the wide sloping lawn behind the vicarage, the boating party was landing, and Darlington was nowhere in sight. The ladies had come down from the rose garden, and Ellen was loudly lamenting the soaking her gown had received in the heat of the race. There was the noise and confusion that always attended a Shaw gathering so that Bel and the earl were hardly noticed, except that Bel's mother cast them a sharp glance, and Auggie stared at Bel on the earl's arm. Kit and Sarah, running up, crying "Auntie Bel," gave her a ready excuse to leave the earl's side. He let her go with a simple bow. She stayed with the children, helping her sister-in-law coax them into the house and into their carriage.

She believed her encounter with the earl had escaped scrutiny. Then, on their return to Shaw House, as she mounted the stairs to her room, her mother called.

"Isabel."

The quiet firmness of her mother's voice made Bel turn. The knowing gray eyes were upon her.

"I'd like to speak with you tomorrow morning after breakfast, in my sitting room, please."

10

NICK WOKE FROM a dream in which he lay kissing Bel Shaw, her white gown spread against a bed of sweet crushed grass. He groaned and lay still, willing his heart to slow its tempo, his heated body to cool. What a fool he was to have gone to that dinner. He knew the inescapability of his own desires. He was his parents' child after all, and he should have known—*had* known in some recess of his mind—that seeing Bel Shaw would stir him.

"Nicky, run along, Mama's busy." His mother's words came back to him, spoken as often as not from the embrace of one of his tutors. They had been a singularly handsome group of young men, who had spent as much time in his mother's bedroom as in the schoolroom. The wonder was that one of them had actually found the time to teach Nick to read. Left to his own devices, Nick had wandered the house, often finding his father similarly engaged elsewhere.

As he grew older, he had become so perfect in discretion that he could pass through these scenes for a book or a meal or whatever he needed without disturbing his parents or their guests in the least. He had come to believe himself invisible in his parents' household until the summer he turned fifteen. That was the summer he had discovered how powerful his own desires could be.

One of his parents' male guests had been called away, leaving his partner, a widow, unattended. She had had a love for the pianoforte, and Nick had been ordered to turn the pages of her music for her, patiently observing the rise and fall of her creamy breasts and enduring the brush of her sleeve against his body.

Then one afternoon he had been sent to the widow's room to return a shawl she had left in the garden. At her bidding he had entered to discover her rising from her bath. It was only later that he realized how contrived that meeting had been. The widow had nearly completed his seduction the afternoon his parents had been drowned, but their deaths had ended the party, sent all the guests seeking gayer quarters elsewhere.

But he had learned about kissing, and the knowledge, once gained, had not been easy to put aside. It had haunted him in London; it haunted him now. But he no longer saw the breasts of the temptress, now he saw Bel Shaw's mouth, her chin, her eyes, the curls about her face.

He would kiss her. If she had the power to disturb his sleep, to render him witless, then he would have to kiss her. But he could not let himself be caught by such kisses. He would have to set some limit, keep some check on his own desires so that he did not become what his parents had been. This much he had decided sometime between the last owl's screech and the first cock's crow.

In her blue sitting room Serena Shaw had all the authority and dignity her husband possessed upon the bench. That her children were seldom called to the room lent a further awfulness to the occasions when they were. Bel herself had not been called for years, not since her fourteenth summer, Tom's last summer at home.

Her mother sat embroidering white on white, a collar for Diana, her elegant hands swift but unhurried, her whole person placid, as unruffled as a still morning. Bel seated herself opposite and waited.

"My dear, when you behave in a manner uncharacteristic of yourself, I must take note and wonder at it," her mother said. "Is something troubling you?"

"No, of course not," Bel replied, sure that if she said it rapidly enough before there was time to consider, it was not precisely a lie.

"Then, my dear, I find it hard to understand why you, who have such scruples, should have started a rumor about the village that our new neighbor was ill. For that is what I have heard from too many to doubt its truth."

"I meant no harm, Mother."

"I understand that no fewer than a score of persons called upon the earl in a single afternoon, not to mention others later in the week."

"Surely there was no harm in their showing him such kindness?"

"Ah, but perhaps he did not wish his privacy so . . . so invaded. He is in mourning, after all."

"Perhaps he did not."

"And did you know that William and Price called upon him?"

"No." The mention of these two poor old soldiers who had been languishing for want of work since the war and who could not have made the trip up to Courtland easily caused Bel to spring up and turn from her mother.

"Do you suppose the earl was the more pleased or the more offended by his callers?"

"I really couldn't say, Mother."

"Ah. Which do you suppose is the wisest course in regard to such a man, a man of power and influence beyond even the boundaries of Ashecombe?"

"Why, honesty and courtesy."

"Just so," said her mother.

If Bel's interview with her mother had wounded her conscience and self-regard, her next interview promised to be still less endurable. She had been sent with Auggie as a companion to apologize to the earl. Serena had made it clear that nothing could excuse Bel from this duty or justify any delay. The ponies were hitched to the cart, and Auggie called from the schoolroom. He sulked at her side, halfheartedly guiding the ponies and shouting encouragements to Honey, who trotted alongside, occasionally annoying the ponies.

"I thought you hated the earl," Auggie complained.

" 'Hate' is too strong a word. I am indifferent to the earl," she replied.

"Then why were you hanging on his sleeve last night?"

"I was hardly hanging on his sleeve. I had to accept his help, that's all."

"You had to? Hah!"

"Well, I did."

"Why?"

"Because of Darlington, that's why."

"Oh." Auggie averted his eyes.

"Is that all you have to say? I thought *you* hated Darlington."

"Not anymore."

"Well, I wouldn't trust him, Auggie. He's angry with me and like to take it out on you and Arthur."

"I don't think so."

"Why not?" She looked directly at her brother, but he would not meet her gaze. "He has before."

"Never mind." She sensed Auggie was hiding something from her, and she was tempted to press him for his secret, but they were approaching

Courtland and her mind was full of her impending meeting with the earl.

In the face of her mother's wisdom, Bel's behavior toward the earl appeared childish and unworthy of her training and her family. Furthermore, if she had offended a man who had it in his power to employ a good many people of Ashecombe who had been hungry for want of steady work ever since the war's end, she had behaved badly indeed. But what of his offenses? How could she explain to her mother the man's power to make Bel seem in the wrong and the Shaws appear rude and dishonest?

When the ponies drew the cart to the top of the earl's drive and Bel saw the bustle of activity about his manor, she felt the weight of her duty to the Shaws and the village press all the more heavily upon her conscience. It seemed the earl had hired dozens of men. Some were employed in removing ivy from the windows of the manor. Others were trimming hedges and scything the grass. Still others were on the roof of the stable, which was exposed to its framework of beams. As Auggie reined in the ponies, four men hefted a great beam onto their shoulders and carried it to a sling at the base of the stable wall. Two men slipped the sling around the beam while others on the roof began to pull at the ropes which lifted it. The strength and briskness of the men made the work look effortless. As the heavy beam rose in the air, the men on the ground stepped back, and at the sound of the ponies' hooves, they turned.

Bel gave a little gasp.

"What?" said Auggie.

"Haverly," she said. He had been one of the men carrying the beam, and now he was coming toward them, his quick stride closing the distance too rapidly for Bel to prepare herself. He was very much the shepherd again in his shirtsleeves and corduroy breeches and old boots, his dark hair wind-ruffled.

The dog bounded up to him, wagging her tail and barking a friendly greeting, until a curt command from Auggie brought her back to the pony cart.

"Good morning, Miss Shaw," said the earl, holding up a hand to help her down from the cart. He merely nodded to Auggie. "What brings you here?" he asked Bel. She put her hand in his and stepped down from the cart, pulling back from his hold as soon as her feet touched the ground.

"May I have a word with you?" she asked.

" 'But one word?' "

The line was familiar though she couldn't place it and she forgot to try, for the earl was grinning at her and she had never seen his face lighted by a smile before. His eyes flashed with a sparkle that made her think of the wooded stream below catching errant beams of sunlight, and for a moment she forgot her purpose. The clip of shears and the rustle of ivy vines falling as the men working on the manor exposed brick and stone recalled her to her situation.

"Must we speak here?" she asked.

"Would you care to step inside?"

She nodded. It would be so much easier to speak to him without an audience.

"And your brother?"

Auggie—she had forgotten him. She had no desire for him to hear what she meant to say. "Auggie, will you wait? I won't be long." He was slouching on the cart seat with a long-suffering air, but his eyes were sharp with wary curiosity.

"Shaw," said the earl, "you may take your ponies around behind the stable. Ask for Farre. He'll see that they're taken care of."

Auggie's look hardened resentfully, then he shrugged and set the ponies in motion. The earl offered his arm, and Bel accompanied him through the wide door set in stone and topped with a modest pediment. Inside, two girls from the village were dusting the rails of the great stair. The earl opened a door on the left and stood aside for Bel to precede him.

She stepped into a square white room with bare polished wood floors, brightened by two patches of sunlight from the tall, north-facing windows. There was the faint odor of paint and polish. Shelves lined the far wall, filled at one end with books. More books lay in several open crates on the floor. The earl was clearly unpacking an extensive library, and Bel could not help a little exclamation of pleasure at the pretty room.

"I do read," he said, smiling wryly now. "Would you care to sit down, Miss Shaw?" He crossed the room to one of two chairs before a fireplace on the interior wall.

"No, thank you," she said, recalling her purpose. He nodded and returned to face her. They stood in the center of the room, the sunlight at their feet, her back to the books, his to the door. He was looking at her in that way he had that quickened her pulse. She was uncomfortably aware that with the brown trim of her straw bonnet and brown fringe of her shawl opposite his brown breeches and dark hair they looked like a matched set of pastoral figures.

"Did you tell my father you suspected my brothers of the attacks on your property?" she asked.

She could see she had taken him by surprise. "No," he replied, "but your father's investigation will be quite thorough. If your brothers are the least guilty, they will be found out."

"If they are named, will you insist that they be brought up before the law?" Again she saw in his eyes that her questions had surprised him.

"Is there some reason I should not?"

"My mother has sent me to apologize to you."

"Ah," he said. "You wish to trade an apology for a

promise from me to forget the injuries your family has done me?"

"No, I do not. I do not wish to make any apology to you." She took a deep breath. "But I am willing to make amends for any trespassing my brothers might have done."

"Amends?" He turned from her, a speculative note in his voice, and stepped to a large desk in front of the windows. He stood with his back to her, straightening some papers on the gleaming surface. Next to his hand lay an old green cap of Auggie's.

Oh, Auggie, Bel thought, *what have you done*? "Yes, amends," she continued. With the evidence he had against the Shaws he would certainly not make this easy for her. "Perhaps I can render you some service. I could tie flies for you. I know all the hatches on the Ashe. I could put your kitchen garden in order or your books. I . . ."

He turned to her then, leaning his hips against the desk and crossing one booted foot over the other. "No," he said, "thank you. I am quite competent to do the things you suggest, and each is less a labor than a pleasure."

"Is there nothing . . ." she began, looking down, dismayed at his refusal. She twisted the ends of her shawl around her fist.

"There is something." His voice, low and intense, alerted her to a change in him, and she looked up. "You could kiss me," he said. "A kiss for every trout your brothers have cost me." Her eyes met his, and she felt her cheeks heat.

"You can't be serious."

"But I am."

"A lady can hardly agree to such an arrangement, and you are no gentleman to suggest it." She pulled the twisted ends of her shawl tighter around her hands.

"I know. Nevertheless, it's kisses I want from you."

"You think because I've been kissed before that I will kiss anyone, that I am light-behaved and have no honor to be lost?"

"No, I think you'll kiss me because you love your brothers." His gaze, level and steady, held hers.

"You are no better than Darlington."

He winced at her words. "I suspect I am worse, but if you kiss me, I won't tell. Our bargain will be just between us."

"And if I refuse?"

"You will have to depend on my good nature and generosity in dealing with trespassers."

"To offer me such a bargain, you can have none."

"Exactly," he said.

"How many fish do you imagine my brothers have cost you?"

"Would you believe a thousand?"

She gasped. "A thousand!" He wasn't serious. Then the implication of the words hit her. He wanted a thousand kisses from her. Her cheeks burned. She shook her head.

"No?" he said hoarsely. "Would you believe a score?"

She shook her head again, not trusting her voice.

"A dozen?"

It was impossible to look at him, impossible to look away. She nodded.

"We have a bargain then? In exchange for a dozen kisses from you, I will bring no action against your brothers for any damage they might have done to Courtland or my stretch of the Ashe."

Again she nodded. His dark eyes on her were their deepest, blackest.

"I want one now."

She took a step back. How had she agreed to such a bargain?

"Just one," he said.

She didn't move.

He pushed himself up from the desk, crossed the short space to her, and pulled her hands out of the tangled fringe of her shawl. He backed to the desk, keeping their gazes locked, and pulled her gently along. He lifted her hands then and placed the palms against his chest. A tremor went up her arms as she felt the firm muscle under the thin shirt. His heart was racing; she could feel its mad tempo with the heel of her palm.

"I haven't much cared for kissing before," she told him. He was undoing the ribbons of her bonnet, pushing it off her head to dangle down her back. Then his hands went to her waist, and he nestled her lightly between his legs.

He swallowed as if his throat were dry, and reached up and covered her hands with his own. "Push against me if I don't stop," he whispered. "I do mean to keep this bargain." He lifted his hands to her face, gently framing her cheeks. "Close your eyes," he suggested.

She let her lids close and felt him pull her face toward his.

His lips touched hers lightly, and she heard his breath catch in his throat. Then the warm firm mouth pressed against hers more strongly, breathing wonder and passion into her, so that her knees gave as if there were no strength in them, and she leaned into the hard chest under her fingertips.

Almost at once he lifted his mouth from hers. His hands dropped to her waist and clung, and he lowered his forehead to her shoulders. She felt his breath warm and ragged against her breast. When he had steadied his breathing, he raised his head and set her aside. He turned away and strode to the door, then stopped, his hand on the knob. Over his shoulder, he said, "I will find Auggie and have him bring the cart round for you." He paused. "Your brothers will have little to fear from me, Miss Shaw, if you can keep this ... sweet bargain."

Monday evening

Dear Tom,

I know you must have reverses and losses from time to time, and yet you have spared us the most painful aspects of these encounters. So I shall spare you my defeats. Indeed I hardly know how I can explain what has happened to-day. Pride and folly have led your sister to a most foolish bargain with Haverly. He now has both your brothers and your sister in his power and can quite embarrass the Shaws should he wish to.

I know you would counsel me to appeal to Papa, but I cannot. Surely I am of an age to extricate myself from difficulties that are the consequence of my own actions. Besides, with the coming trial of the Hilcombe villagers, Papa and Mother are depending on me to manage matters at home. What a mull I've made of it!

Did you know how much the hanging of John Cashman affected Papa? He was in London then, and your ship was in action, your letters full of the valor of common men. Since then the thought of any that have served the country being so unjustly treated as Cashman was has haunted him. In this Hilcombe case are some three men who were in the army and discharged without pay or credit. You can imagine, then, how Papa is determined to save them, how necessary Mother is to all his ruminations and notes.

A sober letter, is it not? You will not want another if I continue in this vein. So I must tell you that Fanny and Louisa have arrived. They have more *beaux* than bandboxes. It is true; we have been given a most complete accounting. A gentleman with five thousand a year has called upon Louisa, and Fanny has received particular attentions from an "honorable." How am I to bear such conceit when you are not here to share a moment's wicked amusement at their expense?

But what is London. It is so still and sweet a night in Ashecombe that I would be the Ashe itself and wind my way in secret through the wood to hear the faeries at their play and steal perfume from the sleeping flowers. Dearest Tom, trust me, I will come about, though Fanny and Louisa smirk and sneer and the earl demands his pound of flesh.

As ever,
Isabel

11

NICK LAY ON the pebbled bank at the edge of the wide shallow pool where he had first encountered the Shaws, and considered whether in making his bargain with Bel he had won or lost. The Ashe, like some sleek, black night creature, slid past his outstretched legs. The air thrummed with insect harmonies, and hovered over him, a fragrant balm of clover and meadow grass, honeysuckle and musk rose, without so much of a stir as might be dignified by the term "breeze." But this was not the wood of Athens where the fairy queen slept in a flowery bed, her eyes enchanted by a magic flower, and woke to fall in love. No amount of wishing would bring Bel Shaw to share this fragrant bank with him. He stretched and shook off the fancy.

Bel would be in some bright room of her family's stone house, the voices and laughter of a crowd of relatives rising about her in a loud jumble of sound. He would be wise to imagine her at this moment, despising him. She had said he was no better than Darlington. She had implied that he had neither generosity nor honor. He supposed she was right. The moment in his library when she saw and recognized the evidence he had against her brothers—that had been the moment to be generous, but he had not been thinking then of her good opinion, only of her beauty. He could call upon her and release her from their bargain. His conscience prompted it. But the voice of conscience could not check the elation that swelled inside him as he let himself recall the kiss he had bargained for.

Here, with only the stars to witness his folly, he could safely remember the press of her hands against his chest, the softness of her cheeks under his fingers, her lips yielding to his. None of the kisses he had shared with the widow in his fifteenth summer had prepared him for Bel's kiss. Those other kisses had been calculated to rouse him to mindless sensation-seeking. Bel's kiss had been aware of him, not playing upon him, but attending to him, as if she had been alert in every sense, as if she had been waiting to hear just what he had to say, as if she had been holding her breath, watching for some eagerly awaited sign in the heavens. No doubt the gentleness and wonder of it all would be transmuted in his dreams into something as base and carnal as he was. He should release her.

But he would have just one more kiss before he did.

Bel had long since learned that taking Fanny and Louisa to the village was a cross between amusement and penance. The carriage must be brought out, of course, for such gowns and slippers as her cousins had brought from London could not stand the injuries of walking the lanes of Ashecombe. And the effort of examining and condemning the village's few shops would be so fatiguing as to require some refreshment in the inn's one private parlor. Then they would have to call upon Aunt Margaret at the vicarage to relate the shortcomings of the inn's bill of fare. The whole adventure would end in Fanny and Louisa retiring for a nap, though each would readily claim that she could dance all night in a close ballroom in London without feeling the least weary.

They were approaching the inn, and Bel was com-
forting herself with the thought of two or three of the
choicest comments of the morning that she might
share with Tom, when the earl emerged from the inn
door. He was the shepherd again in a loose white
shirt and buckskin breeches, a wide-brimmed, flat-
crowned country hat low on his brow. He strode into
the sunlight and stopped abruptly when he saw her.
Her cousins, full of their complaints, strolled on, as if
unaware of the young rustic beyond the tips of their
elegant noses, but Bel could not take a single step.
Whatever the earl's business had been in the inn,
whatever had occupied his mind and made his stride
so purposeful a moment before, appeared to be forgotten as he looked at her. In his dark eyes was the
memory of their kiss.

She could not doubt it, for in the same instant, her
senses awoke. Her lips, her skin, her very blood remembered that brief touch. The comfortable certainty
with which she had assured Tom she could defy
Haverly dissolved. The heat of betraying color rose
in her cheeks, and she felt again the unreasonable
pull of his person.

"Bel, are you coming?" demanded Fanny, looking
first at Bel, then at the earl.

Conscious of Fanny's scrutiny, Bel pleaded with
her eyes, *Don't let her see what I see*, and the earl,
seeming to understand the warning, turned to look
over his shoulder at the inn.

The door opened again and Haverly's servant
stepped out, laughing at some sally from within.
"Nick, lad," the man called out, "Pratt says he's a
lass will do . . ." Catching sight of Bel and her companions, he stopped speaking, nodded to them, and
turned back to catch and hold the door.

Fanny and Louisa moved forward, accepting the
man's courtesy as their due, but Bel looked down
and drew a steadying breath. Haverly's gaze would

follow her cousins. Their smart spencers, jaunty chip-straw bonnets, and delicate sprigged muslins came from the fashionable world he had left behind. It had been madness the day before that had led him to ask for a thousand kisses, to bargain for a dozen, to take one. She could breathe easily. She had no reason to think he would hold her to their bargain now. She had only to lift her eyes to see whether he would prefer Louisa's sweet, plump prettiness, high color-ing, and heavy copper-gold curls or Fanny's elegant oval face, creamy skin, and regal features.

But when she looked up, she found Haverly's eyes on her, telling her as plainly as if he had spoken that he would claim another of the bargain kisses. Bel pulled at the ends of her shawl, twisting them about her hands, then halted the motion, conscious that just the day before she had betrayed herself with the same gesture until his hands had stopped hers. He moved toward her.

"Bel." It was Louisa who called this time. "Oh, dear, am I interrupting?" she asked, glancing at the earl with a puzzled air. At that Bel whirled and hur-ried up the few steps to the inn door.

Mr. Pratt, the landlord, accustomed to the airs of the Misses Shaw of London, greeted them with un-daunted cheer and ushered them into the private parlor. In a very few minutes they were settled at a table with a clean, well-mended cloth and a clear view of the earl and his companion riding up the street.

"That man meant to speak to you, Bel, I'm sure," said Louisa, her eyes wide at the impropriety of it.

"I don't think so," said Bel. Her cousins had al-ready heard of their new neighbor, his rumored wealth, and his elegant good looks, but Bel was sure they could not see the arrogant Haverly in the shep-herd who had stared at her in passing.

"But you do know him, don't you?" said Fanny.

"You know everyone in the county, I daresay. He's one of Uncle's tenants, perhaps?"

"He's not one of your *beaux*, Bel!" said Louisa.

"No, he's a stranger, really," said Bel. It was small comfort that her worldly cousins could so mistake the identity of the man. She could not quite meet their gaze, or believe that she, Bel Shaw, was compelled to lie to them to protect her honor. She willed the earl and his man to disappear from view.

"Well," said Fanny, "I suppose you are used to such persons addressing you."

"I am used to greeting my neighbors of whatever rank, Fanny. Ashecombe is a small place, after all."

"I daresay the man was so impertinent because he's handsome. A handsome man always thinks more of himself than he should. Did Louisa tell you of Sir James Criswell?"

"No," said Bel, turning to the other girl, and Louisa, straightening her lovely shoulders, leaned forward. For once, Bel could be grateful that her dear village was of so little importance to her grand cousins.

If Nick thought his brief encounter with Miss Shaw in the village had escaped his companion's notice, he was forced to abandon the notion two days later. They had stopped the day's work early to take advantage of a fine evening and a new hatch on the river. Farre was silent as they prepared their rods and lines, but there was an intensity to his silence that told Nick his friend was turning over a problem in his head.

Nick had avoided Farre as much as he could from the moment he had made his bargain with Miss Shaw. He had needed time to subdue the elation that filled him whenever he thought of it, and time to cease to think of it every moment. Then he had had to consider their meeting in the village—Miss Shaw's

surprise at seeing him, the way she had stopped as
suddenly as he had, her apparent inability to move,
the pleading look she had sent him—which she
could not have sent without understanding what his
own glance had meant to say—and her turning away
when she must have seen how eager he was to speak
with her.

Farre took his stand along the bank below Nick's
favorite spot and made the first cast, landing the fly
in a quiet pocket of water. Nick positioned himself
above his favorite pool and watched the swift pas-
sage of a leaf across the surface. There was a fast drift
to contend with, a greater challenge. He had his arm
raised and cocked, ready for the first cast, when
Farre spoke.

"Was that the cut direct?"

Nick checked his movement, but he did not pretend to misunderstand. A long sliver of silver shimmered under the surface where Nick had been about
to cast. "Farre, where did you ever hear of the cut direct?"

"Know more about it than your lordship, perhaps."

"No doubt." Nick kept his eyes on the trout under
the surface and a cloud of insects hovering over the
water in a narrow shaft of light. When he judged
Farre to be busy with his own line, Nick made a cast.
The line arced out over the water and dropped the
fly with its concealed barb into the midst of a dozen
harmless, drowning insects.

"Did you tell her you meant to accuse her brothers
of poaching?"

"Yes." In spite of himself Nick jerked his line.

"Well then."

"I haven't accused her brothers, and she knows it."

"And she knows you might. Blackmail, if you ask
me." Farre made another perfect cast.

Nick had no answer. Farre's words were too near

the truth. But getting Bel Shaw to kiss him will-ingly—he knew no magic to accomplish that. It would be safer to hold her to their bargain.

"I didn't lie to her."

"It doesn't look as if you're going to get much chance to tell her any truths either."

"I will see her again."

"And get the cut direct?"

Suddenly Nick had a bite. His line straightened, and the rod bowed as the fish dove and headed downstream. Nick pulled in, playing the trout along, working it away from the narrow lip of swift water at the lower end of the pool. Farre put down his own tackle and moved into position with the net. Nick struggled on, exerting a steady pressure that drew the fish toward the shallows, anticipating sudden moves that would allow the trout to tear free. As the line that separated them grew shorter and tauter, the fish jumped twice, then dove toward Nick's feet, turned abruptly, and arched out the water, wrenching free.

"Lost a good one there," said Farre.

Nick took a deep breath. "Farre, sometimes you make me think there would be advantages to being as supercilious as Uncle Miles."

"So you'd like to be 'my lorded' a bit. Well, that's a thing Miss Shaw's not like to do. Now those other two we saw in the village—fine London ladies, I think. That pair will toady to you some."

Nick began to strip his line and consider which fly to use next. Vaguely he recalled that Bel Shaw had been accompanied by two other young women. "No thanks."

"Then I don't suppose you're interested in the card that's come from the squire today. Fancy piece of pa-per, too. Looks like the squire might be giving a ball."

Nick was not so foolish as to look up. "I don't dance."

"You look fine in an evening coat, and I'll wager you can walk a girl along a garden path as well as the next fellow."

Blackmail, Nick decided, was more common in human intercourse than philosophers or prelates would care to admit. He could picture Alan Darlington leading Bel Shaw down some grassy path in the fading evening light and knew he could not allow the squire's son such an opportunity.

The Midsummer's Eve ball given by the squire and his lady promised to be a singularly frustrating experience for Miss Fletcher, who was trying to settle whether she should be more pleased that her London cousins would be there to say what was or was not fashionable and look down their noses at the squire, or more dismayed that their dresses were so much finer than the remade gown she was to wear.

"Ellen's dress must have a better border. Don't you think so, Louisa?" said Fanny, staring quite critically at the gown Ellen had flung across Louisa's bed in the Shaws' pretty yellow guest room, where the girls were to dress later for the ball.

"Oh, yes," Louisa readily agreed, "the color is nice enough, almost a willow green, but we should get Beckwith to add that lace from Grafton's."

"What will you wear, Bel?" asked Fanny. At the question the three girls standing beside the bed turned to look at Bel, who sat at a small worktable intent on gathering a length of lace.

"Oh, I've a white jaconet that will do."

"Bel," said Ellen, "not the white. Don't you wish to be truly elegant tonight? The earl will be there."

"I doubt it," Bel replied with only a slight hesitation. "The man is above his company." Since the arrival of the squire's invitation, Haverly had been introduced into conversation too often for Bel's comfort. Each time she found it necessary to busy herself with some trifling activity. This time she held up the length of lace she was working on to check the evenness of the gathers.

"But he *will* be there," Ellen continued, addressing her other cousins. "Darlington told me himself. And besides, the earl came to Shaw Sunday dinner. We all sat at table with him. I'm sure he quite likes the Shaws."

Bel looked up at that moment to protest Ellen's foolishness and saw her London cousins exchange a complacent, pitying glance that severely taxed her patience. She jabbed her needle into her lace.

"I wonder that we never met him in London," said Louisa, moving languidly to the dressing table and glancing briefly in the mirror. "We met so many gentlemen."

"Well," said Fanny, "it would be helpful to know something of the man before one is faced with an introduction."

"The squire will have *Debrett's*," said Ellen, "but I'm sure you will find Lord Haverly a very proper earl. His coats are ever so fine."

Again Bel caught the quick exchange of glances between Fanny and Louisa.

"I hope so," said Louisa, "for it hardly seems there will be enough company for a proper ball. Which of your *beaux* will be there, Bel?"

It was inevitable, Bel thought, that her cousins, having exhausted the subject of their own admirers, should finally ask about hers. The only awkwardness lay in the image of Haverly that came to her mind and left her speechless.

In the silence Ellen giggled. "Bel doesn't have any *beaux*."

"No *beaux*?" Louisa's eyes were at their widest.

"None," said Ellen. She skipped across the room

and snatched the lace from Bel's hands. "John Lyde has gone and got himself engaged to Emily Pence, and Bel says Darlington's not her *beau* either."

"Ellen," Bel protested. Swift and nimble from playing with her brothers, she quickly recaptured the stolen lace. She strove for a light tone. "You know I never counted either of those gentlemen a *beau*, so I can hardly be slighted by Lyde's choice. As for Darlington, I'm sure he's gentleman enough to wish to dance with us all."

"But how dull," said Ellen. "I want someone to dance with me who cannot think of another. Like Lyde and Emily." She paused and when the others looked her way, announced, "I've seen them kissing."

"She allows him to kiss her?" said Louisa, with every appearance of being properly shocked.

"Yes, I saw them just—"

"Ellen," Bel protested in earnest this time, "you shouldn't repeat such things. It might hurt Emily's reputation."

"Don't be so stuffy, Bel. What can it hurt? They will be married soon, and they do kiss so much I'm sure someone else will talk if I don't." Somehow, and Bel couldn't be quite sure how, she and Ellen had ended up facing each other across a wide stretch of carpet, and Ellen was glaring at her.

"We're her friends," Bel urged gently. "It isn't right for us to . . . gossip."

"Well, you shouldn't talk at all, Bel. You let Lyde kiss you," said Ellen, casting a sidelong glance at Louisa.

Bel lifted her chin. "That was years ago," she said. "I was Auggie's age, and those kisses were not what a gentleman shares with his betrothed."

"How do you know that, Bel?" asked Fanny, with an arch of one eyebrow that seriously undermined Bel's resolve to keep her temper.

"I don't know *that*, Fanny," she said, "but I hope

the experience Ellen is so eager to have is a great deal more exciting then John Lyde's kisses of five years ago." She paused. "Please excuse me—I will see that Beckwith comes for Ellen's gown."

Bel let the door close on the sudden silence that followed her abrupt exit and leaned against the cool paneled surface. Thus she heard Fanny's next words quite distinctly.

"Bel Shaw is entirely too proud."

"I'm sure she shall be humbled tonight," came Louisa's reply. "That dreadful white gown and no *beaux*."

"I'm sure," said Ellen, "when Haverly sees how fine you are, he won't ever look at Bel again."

Bel pushed away from the door and strode down the hall. She was justly served for lingering to hear her cousins. With the back of her hand she dashed away hot tears. *She*, proud? She, who wore old gowns, who refused to expand the borders of her skirts till they reached her knees, and who would not depend on another woman's labor to curl her hair? She, who would bear the dust and mud of a lane for the pleasure of walking, who would greet her fellow villagers whatever their station in life, and who could boast no *beaux*?

Her steps slowed. It was true. She *was* proud. She had the Shaw pride, and it would sustain her. She would go to the squire's ball. Let Fanny and Louisa and Ellen sneer. Let Darlington and Lyde snub her. Let the earl . . . let the earl choose to bestow his attentions where he would. She would laugh and dance and be merry—though perhaps she should ask her father not for the carriage but for a tumbril.

12

B EL STOOD, A little apart, in a circle of her cousins
and other guests on the terrace of the squire's
hall. Green folds of earth descended to the gleaming
Ashe a half mile below, and beyond the river, haymakers were still at work in the fields. Plainly Nature
had no sympathy for Bel's troubles. Golden light suffused a clear sky. Not a cloud hovered.

Except for the merest civilities her cousins had not
spoken to Bel since she'd left the guest room that afternoon. She considered escaping to the secluded
walks of Mrs. Darlington's garden, off to one side of
the terrace, but rejected the impulse to flee as craven.

All talk centered on Haverly. Her cousins, having
found an account of his properties in the squire's
Debrett's, were attempting to estimate the extent of
his wealth when Reginald Grant arrived. An amiable
young man of modest fortune, Reginald soon persuaded Fanny and Louisa to describe the delights of
London. Bel listened briefly, caught the drift of the
talk, then let her thoughts go where they would as
she looked out over the river and fields. She smiled
at Phillip as he joined them.

"Louisa," she heard him say, "that's not fair.
Ashecombe has some fine houses. I'm sure no gentleman's house in London has a prospect like this." He
flung his right arm in a wide sweep, encompassing

the squire's fields and wooded acres and ending with a smack against Ellen's shoulder.

"Phil," Ellen complained, adjusting her shawl, "don't be tiresome. Ashecombe is nothing to London."

Phillip cast a pleading look at Bel, but Bel resisted the urge to speak in his defense. Any word of hers in his support would only result in Phillip's being snubbed, too.

"Who's being tiresome at my ball?" asked Darlington, stepping into the circle. "Bel? Not allowed. If you're tiresome, Bel, who will dance with you?"

"Not Bel, Darlington," said Phillip, "me."

"Shaw," said Darlington, "are you asking me to dance?"

Phillip reddened and fell silent. Ellen giggled, and Bel frowned, wishing there was some way to shake Ellen out of her mocking temper.

"Who's to dance the first set?" Darlington asked. "I suppose the Miss Shaws of London are promised already," he suggested, turning to Fanny and Louisa.

"Our numbers are uneven, Mr. Darlington," said Fanny.

"No matter," said Darlington, "there are partners enough for all the pretty girls." His glance avoided Bel.

"Is the earl here yet, Mr. Darlington?" asked Ellen.

"He's talking with your uncle."

Ellen spun to look through the open doors of the hall where they were to dance, and Darlington laughed. "Do you fancy him for a partner, Ellen? Am I to be cast in the shade at my own party?"

"I didn't mean . . ." Ellen began, turning back to the group.

"Do tell us about his lordship, Mr. Darlington," said Fanny. "It seems an odd freak for a man with any substantial property to buy old Courtland. The place has been a ruin for ten years or more."

"But, Fanny," said Phillip, "Courtland has the best stretch of river in the county."

"Rivers," said Louisa, "that's all you think about here. I am sure the earl thinks more about the society of the neighborhood than the fishing."

"Perhaps Bel can tell us," said Darlington. "She's quite a close acquaintance of Haverly's already."

At Darlington's pointed pairing of herself and Haverly, Bel stiffened. The others were staring, and the little space that separated her from them now seemed a distinct gap. Pride had enabled her to endure her cousins' slights, the smirks with which they had greeted her appearance in the old white gown, their unkindness to Phillip, but her pride was stirring dangerously now, bringing blistering words to mind. Her hands clenched into fists around the ends of her shawl.

"We have all met Lord Haverly, Mr. Darlington," said Ellen, glaring at Bel. "Bel can't claim to know him better than any of the other Shaws."

"Oh, but she can," insisted Darlington, looking not at Ellen but at Bel.

Bel raised her chin. She smiled sweetly at her host, and in a voice that perfectly mimicked her cousins' London tones, she said, "Why, yes, didn't I tell you, Louisa? Just the other day the earl was saying how much he prefers the solitude of the river to the society of—"

"It's true," came a quiet voice from behind Bel.

She did not turn. She knew the voice, knew from Phillip's startled face and Fanny's sudden alert interest who it was who stood at her elbow.

"Miss Shaw and her brothers have been among my first acquaintances here," said Haverly.

Bel turned then, and her little movement allowed him to enter their circle. She looked up defiantly, but he merely nodded and did not return her glance. If he meant to join in the attack on her character, he gave no sign.

"Miss Fletcher." He nodded to Ellen. "Shaw," he greeted Phillip. "Darlington, will you present your other guests to me?" he asked.

As the introductions were made, Bel glanced at him. He was at his haughtiest, his expression cool and unrevealing. She was sure not even Fanny, who seemed to study him most closely, could find fault with the elegance of his person. He wore a deep green coat over fawn inexpressibles and a cream waistcoat that emphasized the whiteness of the linen at his throat. Nothing in his manner as he spoke to the others betrayed the least awareness of her at his side, though his nearness started a faint quiver deep inside her where she had not imagined there to be any sensation possible.

"I wonder, Lord Haverly, that we did not meet you in London this spring," said Louisa.

"I can only regret it, Miss Shaw," came the reply.

At the sound of the orchestra tuning, Fanny reminded them all that a set was forming. "Our numbers are sadly uneven—unless, perhaps, you would join us, Lord Haverly?"

He did not answer, and Bel glanced at him again, wondering at his hesitation.

"Haverly, you've been offered the pick of the evening with three such ladies unpromised before you," said Darlington, with a careless sweep of his arm that indicated Ellen, Louisa, and Fanny, posed like the goddesses for Paris' judgment. What Paris, Bel wondered, could resist such loveliness?

"Perhaps the numbers might be evened another way," said the earl, turning to Bel for the first time. She met his gaze. He paused. "I promised the squire I would see his bit of river while it is still light. Miss Shaw, would you accompany me?"

Someone gasped, but Bel did not turn to see who it was. Haverly looked as distant as a god, but he was offering escape.

"Of course," she said. He offered his arm, and she took it. The silence behind them as they strolled across the terrace assured her that they would soon be the subject of her cousins' gossip.

Nick listened to the gravel crunch under their feet, let his heartbeat steady, and tried to think of something to say other than the words uppermost in his mind—*kiss me*. She was wearing white again, a gown of some soft cloth that made him think of moonlight on still water. The fringe of her shawl was the blue of her eyes, and her honey-gold hair was done up in a way that let him admire the curve of her neck and the hollow of her throat. He had been wise not to look at her earlier.

The path they had chosen followed the uneven edge of a wood of elm and silver birch and lay in gentle loops like the undulations his settling line would trace as he finished a perfect cast. Strains of music from the opening set drifted out to them on the still air.

Rallying, he asked, "Are you fond of dancing, Miss Shaw?"

"Yes," she answered. "And you, Lord Haverly?"

Nick considered and rejected the truth. "You needn't call me that, Miss Shaw," he said stiffly. "And you must remind me to return you to the ball in good time."

"Must I?" asked Bel. She raised an eyebrow. "And what am I to call you?"

He laughed. "I suppose it's asking too much that you would call me Nick?"

She appeared to weigh the idea. "It is," she replied, suddenly serious.

They walked on in silence until Nick began to develop a distinct aversion for the dry, brittle sound of gravel. Then a new thought occurred.

"Miss Shaw, you did agree to accompany me just now."

Bel nodded.

"And you were aware that one likely consequence of our leaving the group was that we would become the next topic of conversation among those who remained behind."

"Nothing is more certain," she replied.

"Then it is no new resentment that keeps you silent in my company? Merely the old?"

"What *am* I to call you?" she demanded, glancing up at him.

It was a mistake to look into his eyes, Bel discovered, for he had a way of looking at her as if he had quite forgotten the existence of any other person. The quivery knot inside her expanded and sent tremors along her limbs.

"If not Nick, you mean?" He appeared to ponder her question. "I have other names. I have certainly been called other things, few of which I can repeat to you. Farre calls me 'lad' as often as not. There is 'sir,' or, if you prefer, the more contemptuous 'sirrah.' But which of these allows you to express the exact shade of distance and implacable resentment you feel toward me—I cannot advise you on that."

"You are being kind, you know," she said.

He laughed a brief harsh laugh. "Now that's something you have not yet accused me of being. I cannot recall doing a kind act in my life."

"No 'little nameless, unremembered acts of kindness and of love that are the best part of a good man's life'?" she teased.

"Don't let the poet mislead you, Miss Shaw. You know what I hope for, even here among your friends and family. You refused to speak to me in the village the other day on account of it."

Yes, she knew. Their bargain. At the thought of it, certain sensations she had been but dimly aware of seemed to demand her full attention. The brush of her arm against the lean framework of his ribs, the quiver of her fingertips against the tense strength of his arm. She would do well to remember his contempt for her and her family. "Have you had any further attacks on your property?" she asked.

"None."

"But you still hold my brothers responsible for the earlier attacks?"

"I do." He paused. "And *you* still find my insults to your family unforgivable?"

"I do."

The river was just below them now, and across it the haymakers were tossing the last forks of new cut hay on ricks, a pair of sturdy round women in white caps and aprons were setting tankards on a plank table, and a fiddler was tuning his instrument. The squire had provided a celebration for his people as well as his grander neighbors.

"Nature seems to favor the prosaic over the poetic tonight," Nick said lightly, regretting his reference to their bargain.

His companion looked up at him, and he momentarily lost his easy stride.

"This golden light will hardly do for faeries or ... lovers," he explained, "and it is their night, isn't it?"

"But it is early yet, and faeries will keep to the woods, you know. They are far more likely to visit your stretch of the Ashe than the squire's."

"Are there no faeries in these woods?" he asked, looking up at the dark edge of the wood above them.

"Not likely." She laughed. "The squire wouldn't dream of entertaining such company as Oberon and Puck."

"And Titania?" he asked. "The faerie queen?"

But she looked away. "We had best return to the

ball," she said. "If I keep you from the dancing, I shall be judged very harshly by all the other ladies of the neighborhood."

He made no reply.

They turned from the river and began to make their way up the hill. The sky had taken on a rich violet hue, and the lights and music from the squire's hall seemed impossibly distant. Bel thought their gaiety did not beckon so much as suggest a perfect indifference to all those unfortunate enough to be in the dark. At the center of the gay whirl that was the squire's party, more indifferent than all the rest, would be the Shaws. And the earl would see it. He would see at once Ellen's tireless self-promotion, the airs of Fanny and Louisa, the self-satisfaction of her aunts and uncles, and the inattention and indulgence of her own parents. He must not see it. She must raze such an image from her own mind.

She was grateful for the fading light. By the time they reached the turn in the path that led to Mrs. Darlington's garden, she was blinking away hot tears. She kept her mouth firmly shut on a sob that threatened to escape. With the fingers of her free hand she tried vainly to loosen the strings of the reticule dangling at her wrist so that she might retrieve a bit of linen. It was these efforts that drew her companion's attention to her tears.

"Miss Shaw, what is it?" he asked.

She shook her head and slipped her arm from his to reach into her bag for a handkerchief to press to her nose. She would not cry.

He put an arm around her shoulders and drew her through a rustic, rose-covered arch of crossed poles that marked the entrance to the garden. The path beneath their feet changed to grass and led in just a few steps to a tall hedge where they must turn left or right.

"Which way?" he asked. "Is there a bench somewhere?"

She pointed to the right, and he urged her onward. But when they rounded the corner, he stopped abruptly, and she looked up.

Emily Pence and John Lyde sat wrapped in each other's arms, enjoying a very thorough embrace. Bel stepped back, but the pair on the bench started and looked up. For a moment no one spoke. Then Emily drew herself up a little, tugged at a slipping piece of lace, and said haughtily, "We *are* betrothed, you know."

"Please, excuse us," said the earl. He turned Bel around, and they retraced their steps to the hedge. But when she would have left the shelter of the little garden, he shook his head and pulled her along the path, around the other corner, and on until a turning brought them to a high wall. There he stopped and, leaning against the wall, gathered her to him and held her while the tears came.

Her tears were foolish beyond permission, Bel knew. She did not think ill of her family. Whatever the pretensions of Fanny and Louisa, they were superior and well-bred girls. However silly and unkind Ellen had been, she was a young woman of sense. Whatever her brothers had done to the earl's stream, they were honest and loyal. However preoccupied her parents had been, they were just and cared about their neighbors. It was only in the company of this man that her family appeared in a bad light, and she herself appeared impatient and over-proud. The Shaws had every claim to pride. Still the tears came, and in her struggle to overcome them she pressed her face against the earl's taut chest.

When she had regained some measure of control, she straightened and tried to pull out of her companion's arms, but the gentle hold was firm and unyielding.

"Is it our bargain that brings these tears?" he asked.

"No," she said, looking at the fashionable knot of his cravat. Conscious of the warm points where their bodies touched, of her arms caught against his chest, of his hands at the small of her back, of her limbs pressed to his, she sought to right herself, to dispell the intimacy of the moment.

She shifted slightly so that her body did not lean into his, though his arms still encircled her. "Thank you for rescuing me tonight," she said.

"I am glad you see it as a rescue and not an abduction."

"You must not have heard the conversation if you can consider it an abduction." She felt his heart beat against her wrists, meeting her own pulse.

"I heard."

"Then you know. They were being odious, and I . . . I used you to depress their pretensions."

"Use me so any time, Miss Shaw."

She shook her head. "No, you must not be kind when I can't . . ."

With a sudden rough gesture he cupped her chin in one hand and tipped her face up, compelling her to meet his gaze. "Don't think me kind. Not now. Not when I have you in my arms . . . and want your kiss against all reason."

His eyes told her it was true.

"One?" she asked.

"One." With that word, the night seemed to enclose them in a sweet violet stillness, as deep, as magical as a faerie wood. He released her chin and drew her to him again. As he bent his head, she closed her eyes. His lips met hers gently at first, and then as if he meant to offer himself to her wholly and without reserve; in response her lips parted to drink in all that frankness and generosity. At once he paused. She felt a tremor shake him, and he drew back. There was no breath in her to speak. Above her he leaned his head against the wall, and she saw the pulse in his throat pound with the same frantic rhythm that beat in her. He steadied his breathing and looked down at her.

"I meant to release . . . I can't," he said. "One more."

She shook her head. She could not think why she should protest. There was some reason. There were voices somewhere. They were not, after all, alone in the woods but in the midst of—

He kissed her again, offering her a taste of desire so rich and elusive that she must taste more. As fiery and sweet as the confiscated brandy she and Tom had once drunk. She was drowning in it like a summer bee drowning in a single drop of nectar.

Then a voice intruded.

"Bel Shaw, you can't, you can't," said the voice, shrill and plaintive.

Bel shivered and twisted desperately. She was kissing Haverly in the squire's garden and they'd been discovered. He released her mouth, but his arms stilled her struggles with an unexpected strength.

"Don't," he whispered on a ragged breath.

She steadied herself and turned to the voice. Ellen, Louisa, Fanny, and Darlington stood staring, their faces as cold and white as statuary in the darkness. It was not dark enough, Bel knew, to hide Haverly's hold on her.

"So much for your propriety, Bel," said Darlington. "You were too good for a mere squire, but willing enough for a belted earl, I see."

"She can't have him, too," Ellen complained. "She's always had everything."

"Hush, Ellen," said Fanny. "What do you have to say to this folly, Bel?"

She saw them as she had seen them earlier, spiteful

and triumphant in her fall, and knew it would be pointless to defend herself.

"Nothing," she said.

"Well, you can't expect *us* to say nothing," said Louisa. "You can't embarrass everyone and expect us to say nothing."

"But there is nothing to say," came the earl's voice, low but reasonably steady. "We are betrothed."

13

LOUISA GASPED, ELLEN wailed, Darlington muttered something under his breath, and Fanny looked down her nose. But Nick concentrated on the slight shiver of the girl in his arms, and tightened his hold.

It was madness to make a public claim to Bel Shaw, one she herself would soon deny or her parents disallow. But her kiss had stirred him to madness. His generous intention of releasing her from their bargain had dissolved in the sweetness of her response. Even now his heart beat wildly, and he ached to press his body to hers.

He stared at the shocked faces across from him. How much did they guess? Ellen and Louisa looked genuinely perplexed, but Darlington and Fanny Shaw seemed to be measuring him for any weakness.

"I suppose congratulations are in order, Haverly," said Darlington. "Will you be making a general announcement?"

"Do," said Fanny. "There is nothing like an announcement of this kind to liven a ball."

"We had not thought to speak tonight," said Bel, and Nick felt a thrill that she had not denied his story.

"Why not speak tonight?" said Darlington. "The evening is perfect for it. The month of Hymen and Midsummer's Eve to boot."

He looked directly at Nick, as if daring him to refuse. Nick thought it would give him particular satisfaction to smash his fist into the other man's face.

"You *have* set a date?" said Fanny. "The sooner the better, I suppose."

"Fanny!" cried Louisa.

"Well, I simply mean that if they are going to have clandestine meetings and behave in such a way, they will get themselves and all the Shaws talked about."

"I have no objection to a public announcement," said Nick. He ignored a faint "Oh" from Bel. "But I insist on an apology from Mr. Darlington first—for implying there was any impropriety in Miss Shaw's behavior."

"An apology from *me* when you . . ." The big man took a step forward, then stopped abruptly, his fists raised and looking oddly spectral in white evening gloves. Nick steadied Bel and stepped away from her, facing the other man. He let his own hands hang loose and ready at his side as Farre had taught him. "*Let the other fellow make the first mistake,*" Farre had said.

Nick looked steadily at his opponent. The silence lengthened until the hum of insects droned in his ears.

Then Darlington lowered his hands. "Miss Shaw," he said, "I apologize for any offense I might have given."

"Apology accepted, Mr. Darlington," said Bel.

Nick nodded.

"Ladies," Darlington said, turning to the others, "may I escort you back to the hall?"

Nick followed at a distance with Bel. Except for one or two sniffles from Ellen the party was silent, and there was no chance for him to offer an apology of his own to the girl he had embroiled in scandal. He could feel the tightness of her body next to his. When they reached the entrance to the hall, Nick turned to her, hoping for a private word under cover of the music and talk, but she spoke first.

"Please," she said, "we must find my parents."

Then the music stopped, the dancers halted in confusion, and Nick heard Darlington speaking, coupling Nick's name with Bel's. He halted on the threshold, brought up short by the sea of strange faces, the wave of noise. At their worst his parents' parties had never drawn so many guests. For a blind moment he let the din wash over him. Then he thought of his uncle entering a room, and a trick came back to him. He imagined himself looking at the crowd through the wrong end of a spyglass, reducing the dancers to toy size. At the same moment he felt Bel's pull on his arm and moved with her toward Augustus and Serena Shaw.

The noise faded as he and Bel approached her parents, and Nick could sense the heads turning their way, the curious stares following them. His legs moved woodenly. He felt his body stiffen. He did not think he could turn his head, yet the Shaws were just steps away.

They looked uneasy, and their faces suggested an effort to mask surprise. Nick feared their scrutiny more than the gaze of the crowd. These were good people. They would see through the elegant disguise of evening clothes. They would see the man whose base desires were his inheritance as surely as his title. Face-to-face with them, he could think of nothing more than the words he had uttered in the garden.

"Mrs. Shaw; sir; we are betrothed," he said. Gasps and "Ohs" greeted his words, the girl at his side flinched, and silence followed.

The Shaws turned as one to regard their daughter with identical expressions of doubt and hurt.

"Mama, Papa, hug me," pleaded Bel, stepping forward.

At her words, her parents seemed to master themselves enough to give a semblance of smiling approval. Nick was hardly fooled by it. Serena Shaw moved forward to embrace her daughter, and Nick heard Bel whisper, "Forgive me." Mr. Shaw, too, folded his daughter in his arms, then turned to Nick as the ladies in the crowd, led by Mrs. Darlington, surrounded Bel and her mother.

"Young man," said Mr. Shaw, offering his hand, "we have much to discuss." The voice was friendly, but the eyes told Nick that he would be questioned as thoroughly as Augustus Shaw, magistrate, had ever examined the accused. Someone stuck a glass of champagne in his hand, and a few men gathered around him to offer their formulas of congratulation. There was a kind of constraint in these that he found awkward, but at least no one was suggesting he dance with his betrothed. He was grateful to the boy, Phillip, for a warm handshake, and a shy "Congratulations, sir."

It was impossible to reach Bel, to find out what she was saying or how she was answering inevitable questions. And for a while he found himself with no particular occupation other than listening to the talk eddying about him. The men made jokes about the advantages of title and about his stealing a march on everyone in the neighborhood. But as his ears became attuned to the jumble of talk, it was the feminine voices he listened for.

Though most of the ladies still crowded around Bel Shaw, he did not see her cousins in the group. Somewhere behind him he heard Mrs. Darlington say, "It is just as well. There was never enough income there for my Alan. There can be no want of money on the earl's side. He won't mind a dozen or more Shaws dipping into his pockets."

Then there was Ellen saying, "She can't have him. She can't have a title."

And Fanny replying, "Well, she won't. She'll be

quite in disgrace. You, Ellen, will take her place at all
the balls. He has compromised her thoroughly. You
may be sure there have been other clandestine
meetings, but you can't imagine he'll allow a marriage to take place."

Nick clenched his teeth. He discovered that his
hand had tightened dangerously around the fragile
stem of his glass. Bel Shaw had enemies she did not
even recognize, and his words in the garden, spoken
out of an ungovernable impulse to possess her, had
unleashed their envious tongues. He stared over the
heads of those nearest him at the women gathered
around Bel, wondering who in that smiling group
would be listening to Fanny and Ellen before the evening was over.

A little shift in the crowd allowed him to catch a
brief glimpse of Bel's face, controlled, withdrawn,
proud. He would marry her. He would offer his
wealth and rank and name to protect her and make
amends for the harm his desire had done to her reputation. The thought crossed his mind that she
would rather have love than any of the other things
he promised, but he dismissed it. He knew how little
love there was in marriage, and tonight he had heard
women frankly envy Bel her access to his wealth. It
would be better to offer Bel Shaw an allowance she
could spend on her brothers and sister than feelings
she could not return. It would not be easy to insist on
a marriage between them, but he meant to do it.

Lord Haverly had accompanied them to Shaw
House, where they sat in the library waiting for
Jenner to bring the tea tray. It was an end to the eve-
ning that Bel could never have foreseen.

Not a word had been spoken in the carriage, and
only the merest civilities had been exchanged since.
Her mother's calm temperament and her father's
habit of suspending judgment until all the facts were

known, qualities which she had long admired, were now an excruciating trial to endure. Her father apologized to the earl for the disorder of papers and volumes associated with his preparations for the Hilcombe trial. Her mother consulted Haverly about his preference for tea or coffee as an evening refreshment. There was more talk of the upcoming trial and her father's view of the chances for a needed postponement.

There had been no opportunity for her to speak with the earl about the surest way out of their engagement. He sat not six inches from her on a generous settee, and still there was no chance for talk. Though how she would have the courage to speak to him she did not know. Tonight she had kissed him back, kissed him not out of curiosity as she had once kissed Lyde, not out of mild excitement as she had first kissed Tom's friend James, but out of something she did not care to put a name to.

She did not blame him for claiming they were betrothed when the others had caught them in the garden, and she did not blame him for announcing their betrothal later to the whole party, though he had done it coldly and without any thought for the distress of her parents. But now it was time to free themselves, and he had not once looked at her. She could not imagine how they were going to do it without mentioning their bargain, and to mention their bargain meant her brothers were in danger after all. And if her brothers were publicly accused, her father's reputation would be hurt, and his power to defend the villagers diminished. She felt her stomach tighten in a sickening knot.

The tea tray arrived and they were soon balancing saucers and cups, her father stirring deliberately, as if in the motion he would find some explanation of the evening's events.

"Now then," he said at last, "perhaps you will tell

us about this engagement." Her father lifted his gaze and looked first at the earl and then at her. She wished she had some cue from Haverly, some hint of what was in his mind. Her hand shook slightly, rattling her cup against the saucer.

"Perhaps, Lord Haverly, you and Bel have had more opportunities to meet and form an attachment than we had realized?" her mother suggested.

Beside her the earl shifted slightly and placed his teacup on a table.

"No . . ." she began.

"No, ma'am," he said. "We have met just a few times. Miss Shaw has no trysts or rendezvous to blush for or explain."

"Then are you so very sure of your attachment?" her father asked. Bel saw the trap that had been set and held her breath. Haverly would see it and use it to free them.

"Sir, I wish to marry your daughter. I plan to remain in the neighborhood and to improve the house and property I purchased. I will make appropriate provisions for Miss Shaw and any . . . heirs we may have, and her brothers and sister if necessary."

"No!" It was said before she had time to consider. What was he saying? She turned to stare at him, but he would not meet her gaze.

"Bel," said her father, "you don't wish your groom to be generous? Certainly, a careful papa would hold him to the bargain he offers."

At that Haverly did turn to her. Their eyes met, and his told her what he had told her in the beginning—their bargain was just between them. Her brothers would be safe as long as she chose to say nothing. She lowered her gaze from his.

"Is there something we should know?" her mother asked gently.

"Ma'am, sir," said the earl, facing her parents

again, "I have compromised your daughter and have every intention of marrying her."

Her father stood so abruptly that tea sloshed from his cup. He set it down with a force that made the china ring. The earl rose more slowly, but he did not flinch, any more than he had when he faced Darlington in the garden.

"Was this intention to marry formed before or after you compromised my daughter, my lord?" demanded her father.

"Who is to say when such an intention is formed?" the earl replied.

"And if we should refuse the permission you had not the courtesy to seek?" said her father.

"I hope you will not refuse me, sir. I do not like the things that were said about Miss Shaw this evening."

"And I do not like the things you have said to me, young man. You do not even claim to love my daughter."

"Papa," protested Bel, "you must not . . ."

"Bel, better an injury to your reputation than a loveless marriage. Can you assure me of a lasting attachment to this man?"

"I . . ." She turned to the earl, but the haughty profile offered no hint of his thoughts. If it were only her reputation at stake and not her brothers' safety, not her father's power to do a just act. If only she could speak to Haverly alone. She must.

"Your lordship," said Bel's mother, "perhaps a scandal could be averted if you would agree to accept Bel's regrets and leave the district for a time."

"Impossible," came the reply. His countenance did not soften in the least.

Bel watched him, amazed. He could not wish to marry her. She had heard the description of his lands and titles that had so impressed her cousins. And though his opinion of the Shaws was unjust, her family pride did not blind her to the disparity in rank and wealth. She could not imagine a man of his position making a connection with a family such as hers. She could not make sense of his refusal to end their betrothal.

"Have you set a date?" asked her father quietly.

"No."

"If you are determined on this course, we must insist on an early date," her father said. There was silence. The two men faced each other no more than a stride apart—the earl tall and dark with an unyielding rigidity, Bel's father as tall, but fair and with a weight of dignity in his bearing.

"Is three weeks too soon?" asked Haverly.

"Arrogant . . ." began her father, but Bel's mother rose and put a hand on her husband's arm.

"Charles can arrange a special license, I'm sure, unless you wish to be married in Derbyshire," she said to the earl. "Can your family and friends be accommodated here in Ashecombe?"

"I have . . . a very small family," he said.

"We will be pleased to receive them, my lord," said Serena.

"Thank you, Mrs. Shaw," he said.

Another silence followed, the two men still standing, awkward now, until Bel's mother nudged her father.

"Sit down, my lord, sit down," said Augustus, sitting himself and taking up his cold tea, staring into it, then putting it aside. "We should do a toast, shouldn't we?"

"No need to on my account, sir," said the earl. "I will take my leave of you, if Miss Shaw will show me out."

"Of course," said Bel. She stood immediately.

A few strained farewells later and they were in the hall. The earl offered his arm, but Bel shook her head. He gestured for her to precede him. She turned on her heel and took two quick steps, but he seized her elbow, forced her to a moderate pace, and then released her arm.

"Are you mad?" she asked in a low voice, turning slightly to catch his reaction.

"Yes," he said.

She spun and stopped in his path, so abruptly that his unchecked momentum brought them chin to cravat. Bel took a deep breath and stepped back, but too late. He was smiling, and his nearness had already started that unsettling quiver inside her she was coming to associate with his presence. She suppressed it, clenching her teeth and straightening her shoulders, but it shook her nevertheless.

"You may be mad, but I am not," she said. "We would be fools to let three kisses and the malice of others trap us in a marriage neither chose to make."

"So?" he said.

"So, we must talk, plan . . ."

"Now?" The word, uttered in a low voice, made her study him closely. He appeared composed, but she did not trust the look in his eyes.

"Tomorrow."

"When?"

"I cannot get away unnoticed easily," she told him. "It will have to be dawn or late evening."

"Dawn, then. Where?" he asked, as if he were used to making such arrangements every day.

"The big pool?"

"I will be there, Miss Shaw."

He bid her good night then, stepped around her, and left the house without calling for any servant to assist him.

Slowly she made her way back to the library. *Dawn*. She took a deep breath. It was not so very far away. There was no need to say anything foolish to her parents until she and the earl had agreed on their story. In the morning she would convince him that a marriage between them was to be avoided at any cost—and could be avoided with just a little push.

She opened the library door. Her parents were sitting together on the settee she had shared with the earl. "She is too proud," her father was saying. Her mother answered in low, earnest tones. Then both looked up.

"My dear," said her father, rising and coming to give her shoulders a squeeze, "I suspect your mother and I have been too busy about these Hilcombe folk to notice your attachment for this young man. I know no ill of him, and you shall teach us to know him better."

Bel looked from him to her mother. They, too, thought her over-proud. Then there was no one to turn to. She would sort this out for herself and meet the earl at dawn.

Bel shivered and pulled her brown pelisse more tightly about her. Dew-spangled grass along the lanes had dampened her shoes and her skirts. Her toes, even in sturdy half-boots, were numb, and she paced the narrow pebbled beach to keep warm. She supposed she was early for this meeting with him, but she had been unable to sleep. Gray light faintly revealed the green of the leaves. Mist was rising from the pool and the reeds on the opposite bank. In the birds' song she could hear only impatience. If he didn't come . . .

She shivered again and knew it for that other, inner shiver that had nothing whatever to do with being cold. She looked up. Above her Haverly stood at the edge of the wood. And for a minute she half-expected him to lift a reed pipe to his lips and play some irresistible melody known only to shepherds. Then he moved. Mist eddied about him as he descended the path and crossed the gravel strip of beach. She put out a hand to hold him back, and he stopped, but not so far away as she could wish.

"Good morning, Miss Shaw," he said solemnly.

The greeting, formal and familiar, broke the spell. "Good morning, Lor—" She stopped. This was awkward. She dropped her hand. It was more than awkward, and she could not recall precisely how she meant to convince him that they should end their false engagement.

"You wanted to tell me that we should not marry," he said.

"I should not have to tell you," she said. She drew herself up, clasped her hands loosely in front of her, and assumed her most reasonable air. "You do not lack intelligence. We are entirely unsuitable for one another."

"Entirely?" He was being deliberately provoking to look at her in such a way, reminding her of those kisses in the garden.

"Certainly we have no respect for one another, and you must agree that respect is a necessary basis for even the most tepid of marriages."

"Did you wish to contract a tepid marriage?"

"Of course not," she said.

"Then are we not suitable? There's no danger of a tepid marriage in our case, is there?"

"We are unequal in birth."

"Are we? I assure you I am willing to produce a *Debrett's* if it will ease your mind about my birth and connections."

"You are ridiculous." She turned and strode to the river's edge. The first streaks of silver lit the surface. None of her arguments were having the effect she had imagined in the safety of her bedroom.

"Then you should marry me for pity's sake," he said, and for a moment she thought his voice was the voice of a lover.

She stiffened her back and resisted the temptation

to look at him. "Pity is what you'll get from your family and friends for making a *mésalliance*."

"I have ... but one friend, and he's like to say I deserve the worst from you."

"Well, I have many, and ..."

"And they have not all been kind to you. Let me be your friend."

"A friend is not the creation of an hour."

"Let me begin."

"You cannot be my friend and hold my family in contempt."

"I do not hold your family in contempt."

She turned back to him then, met his gaze with a steady gaze of her own, and said, "Then you will release me from our bargain and guarantee that my brothers will be safe from your accusations."

A look of pain crossed his face, and he turned from her to look out over the river. "I did not intend our bargain to injure or embarrass you," he said, "but as it has, let me make amends in the only way a gentleman can."

"But you need not. A man of your power and rank need not feel constrained by conscience to observe such scruples."

"Even a man of rank may want to preserve the character of a gentleman," he replied. He bent and chose a smooth stone from the beach and sent it skipping across the still pool.

"Surely what the people of Ashecombe think of your character need not weigh with you," she suggested.

"I assure you, Miss Shaw, it does not." He turned from the river. "Nevertheless, I cannot release you from our betrothal."

"Then I must run away."

"If you must. But I feel obliged to point out that if you should, as the one who caused you to flee your home I would be obliged to find you."

"Then will you oblige me by leaving the neighborhood?"

"No."

"But you could return to London."

His only answer was a laugh.

"Or your Derbyshire properties."

"No."

"Why do you do this? Do you imagine a marriage to be an amusing interlude, an extended house party . . ."

"No." The vehemence of his reply startled her. He drew a deep breath, apparently needing to compose himself.

"Miss Shaw, you cannot avoid this marriage without causing great embarrassment to yourself and distress to your family."

"Lord Haverly, if you insist on our marriage under these circumstances, you cannot expect it to be a . . . true marriage."

Even in the gray light she caught the flash of surprise and something else in his eyes. She looked away.

"Very well," he said. "But if you cannot fulfill a second bargain, I will yet hold you to the first."

"You will have your pound of flesh?"

"I will."

Friday evening

My dear Tom,

It is my turn to have news. Shaw House is busier even than the deck of your ship on the brink of battle, and the cause is a wedding. This will be the last letter I write to you as Bel Shaw. Tomorrow morning I take a different name.

You are surprised, I know, but what could be less surprising? When a girl reaches a certain age, she is expected to marry, is she not? And her family and neighbors are not to be deprived of the joys of speculating about her prospects or her choice. So you too must speculate, Tom.

But I will not tease you. The man I'm to marry is Nicholas Arthur Seymour, Lord Haverly. There, I will allow you to be surprised at that and to wonder how I came to accept an offer from our arrogant neighbor. What alliance could be more practical than one between neighboring families? I have settled it all in my mind.

You can imagine how much our betrothal has stimulated talk in Ashecombe. People who have not done sums for years have been trying most earnestly to calculate what pin money I shall have. In truth, Papa refused most of the earl's generosity, to the relief of the earl's solicitor. The man was here for a week and managed to appear appalled at every aspect of country life, though I suspect Auggie and Arthur had something to do with the particular discomforts he experienced, including a bat in the bed hangings.

Not everyone is pleased, of course, at this alliance. From the earl's family there has been no word. Only one male relative will attend the wedding. Auggie is cross with me for marrying the man who "stole our stream." And from Fanny, Louisa, and Ellen, I have had nothing but cold looks. They think the title "Lady Haverly" quite wasted on your unfashionable sister, and in that I agree, for I had a title every bit as fine, given me by my parents.

I shall be mistress of Courtland Manor, and the Ashe, our Ashe, shall be mine to fish again. I shall have a comfortable allowance and do fine things for Arthur, Auggie, and Diana.

I have made my bed and now must lie in it as the saying goes. Only, I do wish, dear Tom, that you could be here to laugh with me and dance with me upon my wedding day.

Your sister,
Isabel

14

NICHOLAS ARTHUR SEYMOUR, Lord Haverly, frowned at his reflection in the cheval glass he had added to his dressing room. Even Uncle Miles, had he lived to see this day, would not be able to find fault with the white breeches and the white waistcoat with its tracery of gold sprigs. Nick had only to tie his neckcloth and don his coat and gloves to complete the picture of the elegant bridegroom. Yet every time he looked in the mirror, he had the distinct feeling his bride would not be pleased with his appearance at all. It was the neckcloth that was giving him trouble. He had crumpled three already.

"I've seen men go to Tyburn happier," said Farre, appearing behind Nick and meeting his gaze in the mirror. Farre, too, was dressed for the wedding, for the role of "uncle," a matter of some disagreement between them.

"You look quite lordly," said Nick, holding out a fresh neckcloth. "I could use your help." Farre took the long rectangle of linen from Nick's hand, stepped around to stand in front of him, and began to wind the linen around the stiff points of Nick's collar.

"Chin up, my lord. Let's get this noose around you."

"Farre," said Nick, tilting his jaw up for the older man's help, "don't 'my lord' me. You agreed to come today."

"Not as your uncle," grumbled Farre. "It's a bad idea, your passing me off as family."

"I told Mrs. Shaw you would be there. No one will question it, if she accepts you."

"A dozen folks are bound to recognize me as your man. Then how will things look?"

Nick stared at the ceiling. An army of Shaws would be there at the church to see them married. And just this morning he had been reminded by yet another attack on his stream how little some of them cared to see him wed Bel. It was only fair that he should have someone at his side, someone loyal to him. "If I choose you to stand up with me, what does it matter what the Shaws think?" he argued. "I am marrying Bel Shaw, not her whole family."

"Hmph," came the reply.

Nick knew that tone. Without saying a word Farre always managed to let Nick know when he was guilty of some folly. He had heard that "Hmph" often in the three weeks since he had declared himself betrothed to Bel Shaw.

"Lower now, lad, easy," said Farre.

Nick slowly lowered his chin, putting the final crease in the simple folds of the cravat. He closed his eyes and took a deep breath. It might be madness to hold Bel Shaw to a marriage she did not want, but he had heard enough of the gossip about them to remain fixed on his course.

When he opened his eyes, Farre was watching him closely. For once Nick wished his friend a trifle less shrewd. He pulled his coat from the open wardrobe and handed it to Farre, then turned and extended his arms to slip the jacket on, glad for the excuse to avoid his friend's scrutiny. "What am I going to do about the dancing?" he asked lightly.

"Tell her the truth." Farre slipped the sleeves of the jacket over Nick's hands.

"I'd look a proper fool."

"Limp."

Farre lifted the jacket and Nick shrugged into it. He tried a few lopsided steps and gave it up. "I would forget which foot soon enough."

"Lie."

"Now there's a suggestion in keeping with my character," Nick said dryly. He turned to the mirror and caught a glimpse of his friend's knowing face. "My bride is not precisely eager for this ceremony," he admitted.

"She didn't run away," Farre pointed out. He smoothed the line of Nick's coat.

Nick considered that. It was true, she hadn't.

"Did she kiss you back?"

"What . . ."

"I won't ask you how you persuaded a girl who would neither look at you nor speak to you in the village not days before, to be walking a dark path with you in the squire's garden. But you must know the whole county's been talking about it for weeks."

"I know."

"So did she kiss you back?"

Nick studied his reflection in the glass. She had kissed him back that night in the garden. Twice. He had evoked the memory often to hold his doubts at bay. Of course, those kisses had also ruined his sleep. "She did," he said.

"So," said his friend, "you've put the cart before the horse. Time to put things right. You've got to court the girl."

Nick pulled his watch from the little pocket of his waistcoat and consulted it. "Time to wed her, Farre," he said coolly. "The time to court her has passed." He turned from his friend, picked up his gloves, and left the dressing room.

He gave an approving glance to his bedroom. Paint, carpeting, and new hangings had made the place quite comfortable in three weeks. Next door another chamber, similarly renewed, was fitted up for his bride. He could have no hesitation about bringing her here from her family's fine house. But, looking at the bed, with its gray silk hangings, he could not deny what he dreamed of.

Farre's voice coming from the open door behind Nick stopped him. "Thinking of the marriage bed, lad?"

Nick didn't turn. "Am I breathing?"

"Best not to think of it until you court the lady some," said his friend.

"Farre." Nick faced the other man. "My groom can't be telling . . ."

"But, *your lordship*," said Farre, "today I'm not your groom, I'm your *uncle*, which I'll thank you to remember." He paused and brushed imaginary lint from the sleeves of his coat. "And that allows me to give you a bit of wedding advice, you see. And besides, you'll be needing this." Farre held out a small maroon velvet box, which Nick recognized as the jeweler's box containing the plain gold band he had purchased for Bel Shaw.

"Now, whatever ideas your parents might have given you about love in marriage . . ." Farre went on.

Nick laughed. "Love? In marriage?"

"They must have told you something."

"Farre, there was no need. I *saw*. And there was a widow, who was willing to instruct . . ."

"But you saw it twisted, lad, in greed and revenge. It's love that's got to pull that particular cart, you see."

"And if Bel Shaw finds she can't love me?"

"She will if you let her, if she's free to love you."

Nick met his friend's gaze. There was nothing there to be angry at, only a truth told in kindness. "If I free her, she's not likely to see me or speak to me again."

"You won't know until you try it."

Nick took the box from Farre's hand and opened it. He stared at the band he meant to put on Bel Shaw's finger. "Then I won't know today," he said.

Lengthening bars of shade from towering elms along the edge of the Upper Ashe stretched across the lawns of Shaw House nearly to the wedding party. Nick had been watching their advance for hours.

"I daresay you will think us all quite odd, Lord Haverly," said the woman at his side. "Not Tom, of course, and it is too bad that you cannot meet him, but the rest of us are so used to this . . . this unsettled way. And one does grow accustomed to it. I could tell you when I first . . ."

Just then a small boy and girl in wrinkled white finery with telltale strawberry stains on their collars and sleeves raced between Nick and Mary Shaw, wailing and startling Mrs. Shaw into shouting, "Sarah, Kit!" and momentarily, at least, forgetting whatever she had been about to confide to Nick about the experience of marrying into so large a family. Then the butter-colored Shaw dog skidded into the narrow opening between them, stopped briefly to bark excitedly, jumped straight in the air twice, and ran off in pursuit of the children.

"Oh, dear, my lord, you must excuse me, I must see what my children are up to now." And with that Mrs. Mary Shaw courtsied and, resolutely lifting her skirts for flight, dashed off across the grass herself.

Nick was left standing alone again. The sudden intrusion of small children and large dogs was just the sort of occurrence that seemed to characterize all his encounters with the Shaws. One minute he would be listening to some account of family history, and the next the speaker would have yielded to one of dozens of surrounding distractions and quit, gone off, taken up another topic.

It was at these moments that Nick heard the voices around him fade into whispers, saw heads turn away, saw Darlington at ease, laughing among the Shaws. Each time he would stiffen, would feel the sharp points of his collar against the tightened muscles of his jaw. And he would look for Bel. She was avoiding him. Of that there was no doubt. And he knew why. At the brief, sanctioned meeting of their lips in the church, passion had flared between them scandalously hot, leaving them shaky and robbed of breath. And in the moment afterwards their unguarded eyes had confessed it.

His gaze found her. She stood in one of the bright bars of sunlight, the golden beams caught in the netting of her veil, the satin of her dress gilded. He watched as she pulled a white rose from the garland about her head and handed it to her sister. And he wanted to pluck Bel Shaw from the center of her family and carry her to Courtland. Farre's words came back to him. *"Court her."*

Diana skipped off, and Bel looked up to find her husband's dark eyes on her again. Even across the wide expanse of lawn his gaze started the trembling in her. And with his kiss in the church he had unsettled all that she had settled perfectly the night before.

It had been so clear as she wrote to Tom that she was merely fulfilling the expectations that had always shaped her life and with no sacrifice to her comfort and little to her affections. If she felt a little uneasy, it was only that the unchanging character of village life had led her to believe she, too, was unchanging, and that the suddenness of her betrothal and marriage hardly allowed for the necessary imagining of a new role for herself as some other woman—Lady Haverly. She had concluded that the ceremony in the church would not really alter anything. It would leave her herself. She would merely change her address, have an increased allowance to spend, and join the earl for dinner more often than not.

Then he had kissed her in the church, and she had had a sudden heart-stopping feeling that everything had changed, that if she let him kiss her as he wanted to, she would never be herself again. It had been scary, that kiss in the church, her first kiss since her mother had explained the intimacy of the marriage bed. It had made her heart race and her pulses pound and had stopped her from easy speech with the images it had conjured. She had needed then to surround herself with her family, with people she knew, to hold the earl off. So from the vestry, to the carriage, to her parents' house, she had found others to talk and laugh with.

But wherever she went his eyes followed her, dark with longing. Now as she met that gaze, she saw he meant to cross to her. She looked about for someone to turn to and saw Auggie, his hands in his pockets, sullenly kicking a stone across the lawn. She stole one quick glance at the earl and stepped into Auggie's path. He halted and scowled at her, returning his attention to the stone at his feet.

"Auggie," she said, "won't you wish me well today?" He remained maddeningly silent, and she tried again. "Soon we will be fishing together as we always have."

"Not likely," he said, still looking at the stone he kicked between his feet. "Your husband's not going to allow any more Shaws near his stream."

"Well, he'll have to, if he's my husband and cares about my happiness, for I shall want to see my family often."

"Well, he won't. He's too high in the instep for the likes of us." He raised his head and glared in the earl's direction. "He didn't bring one person from his own family here to meet us."

"But he did. He brought Mr. Farre, a quiet, but pleasant gentleman." Bel turned to follow Auggie's stare. The man she spoke of had stopped the earl several yards from where she and Auggie stood. The two were shaking hands, and then the older man embraced the earl in a hearty and clearly fond way. The scene had all the earmarks of a farewell.

"That fellow?" said Auggie. "That's Haverly's groom."

"His groom? What do you mean?"

"Do you think I don't know? And other folks, too? I met him that day we took the pony cart to Courtland. Darlington knows, he'll tell you. That's no uncle."

Bel considered. There had to be some explanation other than the one Auggie had come to. "If the earl wanted him here today, that can be no insult to us," she suggested.

"That's not what you said before, Bel," he burst out, lifting rebellious blue eyes to hers. "You wanted him to go away, and he would have too, if you'd not *kissed* him and said you'd marry him. Things won't ever be the same, and it's your fault, Bel." Auggie gave the stone at his feet a savage kick that sent it bounding out into deeper grass, and ran off.

She was still staring after him when the earl spoke at her side.

"What is it, Miss . . . Bel?" He was speaking in that kind tone which had proved so fatal to her judgment the night of the squire's ball.

"Who is Mr. Farre?" It was suddenly important to ask.

He did not answer, but glanced away toward the house, where she could see Farre shaking hands with her father. Nearer to them, Aunt Margaret approached with the hasty steps and earnest countenance of a woman with an errand.

Slowly the earl turned back to her, "He's—"

"My dears," called Aunt Margaret, "I've been sent to . . . to . . ." She paused and drew a breath. "Well, I *will* think why I've come. I hope everyone had enough to eat. I hope you did, your lordship. I'm sorry there wasn't more tongue. Men like a good tongue in red currant on a warm evening."

"Everyone had more than enough to eat," Bel assured her aunt, glancing at her husband to see if he were enjoying Aunt Margaret's unintended innuendo. His eyes did not light with pleasure, and Bel faltered. "Even . . . the earl would say so, wouldn't you, my lord?" she asked. He had used her name, but she could not bring herself to use his.

"More than enough, Mrs. Shaw," came the stiff reply.

"Well, I'm so very glad to hear you say so, my lord," said Aunt Margaret, "for no doubt you are used to such grandeur that our dinner seems very poor, although I am sure, in general, Serena's cook presents a very fine table."

"Aunt Margaret, everything was just as it should be," said Bel.

Aunt Margaret sighed. "Yes, dear, it was a lovely wedding. But so sad Tom could not be here. My lord," she continued, turning to the earl, "it is too bad Bel's brother Tom is not here. He's the one in the family you should meet."

"So I've been told," answered the earl.

"So much wit in that boy, and such address."

"So I've been told."

"Of course we're sorry that he can't be here, but he must stay with his ship."

"Yes, ma'am," said the earl.

Bel cast him a quick glance. He was barely civil. She thought his shirt points must be stabbing his arrogant jaw. Aunt Margaret did not show to advantage under his frowning stare, and she certainly deserved his courtesy. After all, he had dined at her table, and he must see how eager she was to please him. Maybe Auggie was right about the absence from their wedding of any true member of the house of Seymour.

Gently Bel asked her aunt about the errand she had mentioned.

"Oh, yes, of course, I remember, the dancing. I came to tell you that you are wanted to start the dancing," she said.

Nick felt a distinct sinking in the pit of his stomach. For just a moment there he had been tempted to speak frankly to his bride, to explain his need for the company of a loyal friend. Now, he must consider what lie could possibly excuse him from the dancing. He offered an arm to each of his companions, and they began to stroll toward the hall, Mrs. Charles Shaw taking up again her apologies for the inadequate banquet they'd long since consumed and adding her hopes that the supper fare would compensate for any earlier disappointments.

Where the lawn encountered the flagstones of the terrace, Charles Shaw stepped out of a crowd of uncles and cousins to claim his wife.

"My dear," he said to her, taking her arm, "have you been asking Bel and her groom to doubt their enjoyment of the wedding feast?"

"Oh, Charles, not for a minute, though I do think there should have been more tongue. No, I was merely saying how sorry I was that Tom isn't there."

Her uncle smiled and winked at Bel. To Nick he said, "Yes, it's a shame, my lord, that you aren't meeting Tom today. He's a fine young man."

Nick merely nodded at this. It was apparently the Shaws' refrain.

"Though I must say, Bel," continued her uncle, "I suspect that if Tom were here, he'd be telling your bridegroom a thing or two about you."

"Then thank goodness I'm spared," she retorted. And Nick could not resist a long look at her. She was so easy with her family. He would like very much to hear her speak that way to him.

"Bel spared?" said her Uncle Fletcher, coming up to them at that moment. "Spared what?"

When it had been explained to him, he laughed heartily and insisted that Bel should not be spared.

"I know just the story to tell about you, my fine niece," he declared. "The story of that time you followed Tom and Alan fishing."

Bel shook her head, but Darlington and several more cousins had joined their group, and a roar of laughing assent went up.

"Give us the story, Fletcher," urged a half dozen voices.

"No, really," Bel protested, "it's not fair. The earl will have no one to tell a story about him."

"Has Farre left then?" asked Darlington.

Nick nodded.

"Shrewd fellow. Where did you find a groom of such talents, Haverly?" Darlington asked.

It was neatly done, Nick had to admit, like an unexpected jab to the midsection. He revised his estimate of Darlington's cunning and jealousy up a notch. " 'There is no telling where the light of talent or genius will break out,' " he quoted, fixing the man with a level stare. He turned to Bel then, but she looked away.

"Let's have that story, Fletcher," suggested Charles Shaw, "or we'll get someone else to tell another."

"Right," said Fletcher, "now listen carefully, Lord Haverly. Once upon a time there was a skinny brown urchin of twelve, who followed two great fellows of sixteen everywhere they went, until one day they decided she could no longer fish with them. But did the lass accept their refusal to take her along? No, she stomped her foot, stuck out that stubborn little chin, and said she was free to go where she pleased.

"So Tom, for he was her brother, carried her up to her room and locked her in. Then the two heartless lads gathered their gear and set off without a care in the world.

"Well, the lass watched from her window until they disappeared over the hill. She pulled the sheets from her bed and two more from the chest, tied one end round the bedpost and tossed the other out the open window, and down she went by way of her makeshift ladder and a stout vine.

"She grabbed her gear and followed the boys' trail until they came to the river. She crossed over and, staying on the opposite bank, came up to the pool where they were fishing. Now, she could see them plain as day, but they had no idea she was there."

Nick stole a glance at his bride to see how she was taking the story. Her cheeks were flushed, but her eyes were bright. She did not look at him, but traded remarks with her cousins, who seemed to know the story well and who added details at will until Charles Shaw called them to order.

"Now the boys had it in mind to get a big trout they had seen," Fletcher continued, "and they took turns casting for him, but he was having none of their offers. Then as Tom was stripping his line, the lass stood up on the opposite shore, cool as can be, made a perfect cast, and hooked that big trout under Tom's nose. Seventeen inches at least, he was. Tom swears he never saw a cast like it before or since."

"Well, she's cast her lures for a bigger fish now, and hooked him, too," put in Darlington. There was a burst of laughter at that and several quick sallies about making an earl bite. Someone slapped Nick on the back.

He felt his body tighten. The image of himself as a gaping trout on a carving platter to be mocked and

served up for the amusement of the Shaws stirred
warring impulses in his breast. He wanted to flee as
fast and as far as he could, as he had fled the mockery of his parents and their guests, and he wanted to
freeze the Shaws, to annihilate them with cold looks
for their thoughtless humor at his expense.

He endured the laughter for another age at least. A
similar story was invented on his behalf, full of exag-
gerated exploits and crediting him with a family he
never had. Each cousin seemed to have some detail
to contribute. Then the sounds of the musicians hired
for the occasion began to draw the Shaws from the
terrace to the hall.

Ellen Fletcher came up, a little breathless and
flushed, to announce, "Bel, if you and the earl don't
come to lead the set, there can be no dancing."

"We shall come," said Bel, turning to him and
looking up.

He stared down at her. Her eyes were full of
laughter and pleasure. She had enjoyed her family's
stories. He would not tell her the truth now for all
the fish or all the kisses in Hampshire.

"You go," he said coldly. "You will find partners
enough." She was as lovely in the candlelight spilling
from the house as she had been in the golden sunset
earlier. He kept his eyes cold, his face rigid, as she
studied him. He was vaguely aware of others staring
too.

"Is this your revenge for my cousins' wit?" she
whispered. "I assure you, their wit was directed as
much at me as at you."

"Take it as you wish," he said. "I will not dance."

Angry pride darkened her gaze, and she seemed
about to make an intemperate remark when Serena
Shaw stepped up.

"My dears," said Serena, "such a public disagreement is likely to be remarked by all. Bel, do join your

father to lead in the set. Haverly, give me your arm for a stroll in the garden."

Bel turned on her heel and entered the ballroom without a backward glance. Nick offered his arm to his mother-in-law.

It was some two hours later that Bel had the satisfaction of seeing her groom enter the ballroom. She was dancing with Darlington. Her face was aching from the smile she had kept in place for each partner, but she continued to laugh and move down the set until the figure of the dance brought her nearly opposite her husband, who stood just inside the open doors to the terrace. One more turn and she could smile gaily in his haughty face. Dipping and bowing, she entered the turn, and coming around to the outside of the figure, she lifted her gaze to his and found there not pride, but an expression so bleak, so bereft of joy, it made her stumble and lose her smile altogether.

A sleepy footman let them in and disappeared at once up the dim stairs with Bel's light case. The rattle of the carriage heading for the stable faded away. Nick regarded his wife as she stood beside him in the entry. Though her head was bent toward the floor and her shoulders drooped a little, and though she had removed her bright veil and covered her satin gown with a sensible pelisse, she did not seem as remote as she had in the whirl of the dancers. He could not help but feel a surge of hope that at last he might begin to make her his.

"Welcome to Courtland, my lady," he whispered.

She straightened and looked at him, her eyes somber and full of doubt.

"At least here," he said, speaking his thought aloud, "there are no Shaws to come between us." He reached out a hand to touch her cheek, but her eyes flashed, and she stepped back.

"You object to the company of the Shaws, my lord?"

Her reference to his rank stung him. "I object to noise and confusion and self-importance wherever I find it," he replied, letting his hand fall to his side.

"And that is what you found today? That is your opinion of my family's efforts to please you—their civility, their warmth and generosity?"

Once again he'd roused her anger, but to hear her defend her family now goaded him beyond endurance. "The civility of the Shaws," he said with deliberate coldness, "consists in regarding a man as a convenient pair of ears into which the whole history of the family may be poured without any consideration for the listener's feelings in the matter."

"And your civility, my lord, consists in feeling your rank so much that you are above your company and above being pleased."

"My rank?" He closed the distance between them as he spoke. "What is my rank compared with the exalted name of *Shaw*?"

"It is my name, my lord. I am a Shaw," she declared, tilting up that stubborn chin so that she matched him glare for glare.

And suddenly he knew the words that would wound her as he had been wounded. "Not any longer," he said quietly. "Now you are Bel Seymour, Lady Haverly."

"If I am, it is only because you wanted your river, because you blamed my brothers for the attacks on your property, because you refused to free us when you might easily have done so."

Bel was surprised at the effect of her words. They had been face-to-face, separated only by their anger, but at her words his gaze dropped, and he turned away from her.

"It's true. I gave you little choice in the matter, but I can free you now." His voice was low, all anger gone from it.

"Free me now? How can you?" she asked.

He turned back to her, but his eyes when he lifted them to hers revealed nothing. "Be my wife, when you wish to be my wife."

"What do you mean?"

"I mean, come to my bed when you are willing and only then. If, after the talk of our hasty marriage has died away, you find you cannot be my wife after all, I will release you."

Bel dropped her gaze from his. His offer dissolved her anger, and she felt again that shaky quiver at the core that his nearness evoked in her. "That seems a wise and generous course, my lord. Thank you," she said.

"Look at me," he ordered, his voice suddenly harsh. When she looked up, he came toward her, speaking slowly and forcing her to step back and back again until she found herself pressed against the wall, and still he moved toward her. "Not *my lord*, not *your lordship*, not *the earl*, not *Haverly*—Nick. Say it. *Nick*."

He leaned toward her, his hands braced against the wall on either side of her face, his eyes on her mouth as if he could compel the word, his lips inches from hers.

"Nick," she whispered.

"And I will have my kisses."

"Now? All?"

He didn't answer at once, and she caught a flash of reckless longing in his eyes before he mastered it. "One," he said.

He pushed himself away from the wall and drew her against him. Her hands slid up his arms to his shoulders as he brought their bodies together. Of all the partners in whose arms she had danced this night, none had the lean strength of him, of muscle and will in harmony. He lowered his mouth to hers, his kiss at first demanding, and then unexpectedly yielding.

He released her and stepped back, his breath uneven. "There's a maid waiting for you upstairs," he said. "Good night." He gave her one last burning look and left the hall. She heard his footsteps cross the gravel drive and fade away. With an effort to steady her shaking knees she began to climb the stairs.

15

BEL PUT DOWN her fork. It was no use pretending an appetite she did not feel. She stared across the expanse of crisp, snowy linen at the place opposite hers, at the gleaming silver and elegant service. The white, pink-streaked globes of peonies she had picked earlier drooped in a low bowl in the center of the table. A fragrant sauce cooled and congealed about the trout on her plate. He would not come.

She had been pushing that thought aside for days. Restoring the dining room had been her first task, begun the morning after their unhappy wedding night. She had begun a letter to Tom, but found herself unable to finish it. She had regretted her part in the first quarrel of her married life almost at once and had needed something to do to let her husband know her willingness to act as his wife in every way—but the one.

The maid who had brought her chocolate that first morning was Susan, a village girl Bel had known all her life. Susan was inclined to a certain cheerful awe at Bel's new position, and her frequent "ma'am's" and "my lady's" left Bel feeling like a fraud. But Susan showed Bel the musty, threadbare dining room and explained that it was not used, that the earl ate in his library or picked up something from the kitchen to take with him about the estate. "His lordship don't like to trouble the kitchen," she confided.

This, Bel soon learned, was an understatement. Her husband preferred not to trouble his household at all.

No matter how early Bel rose, he was gone. Each day he left her a brief, civil note with the housekeeper to say that he'd be about Courtland somewhere and to encourage Bel to do as she wished. The fears that he had roused with his kiss in the church seemed foolish indeed, and the falseness of her situation as mistress of Courtland made her feel awkward with the servants he had hired to do her bidding.

She began to leave messages for him under his door. On the third morning as she shoved her message under his door, she heard the brush of paper against paper. She straightened and knocked lightly. When there was no answer, she turned the knob and entered. Her messages were lying on the floor, untouched. In a fury she had marched down to his library and dumped her letters on his desk, but when she came the next day, her letters remained unopened. She wondered then if he came into the house at all.

If she did not seem to be a wife by day, she was certainly no wife by night. She did not believe he slept in the room next to hers. Or if he did, she suspected him of coming and going through the windows. She would lie in bed in the dark, listening for one sound that would reveal his presence, but her straining ears would catch only her own heart beating.

Then, when she was sure he had no interest in the running of his household at all, he had ordered the lovely tall clock her parents had given them as a wedding gift removed from the hall and placed in Bel's room. Now as she thought of her attempts to please him and his indifference and childishness, her sense of ill-usage grew.

If he knew about the clock, then he must know

about her efforts to restore the dining room. Surely, however pressing the estate business, there was time to have dinner. And surely it would be little trouble for her husband to tell her a time that would suit him.

A footman came in to ask if she wished the candles lighted, and suddenly she could not bear the pretense another minute. She had not said her vows with the understanding that they were provisional in any way. She had accepted his offer of freedom to choose when she would enter his bed because it had seemed foolish to pretend love when there was so much anger between them. Her mother had pointedly advised her against taking quarrels to the marriage bed. But she had not left her home and family and taken his name to be no wife at all. That she could not accept. She would find her husband and demand to know what sort of marriage they were to have. She dismissed the footman, pushed back her chair, took up her shawl, and headed for the kitchen.

A few questions of the cook elicited the information that although his lordship had not been in since early morning, Mr. Farre had returned from Derbyshire and a tray had been sent out to his room off the stables. Bel could not resist one further question. Just who is Mr. Farre she wanted to know. "His lordship's groom, of course. Been with him ever so long," was the reply.

Nick let himself laugh. He tore another hunk of bread from the loaf on Farre's table and reached for a bit of cheese. It was good to have someone to talk to. After the bitter disappointment of his wedding night, it had been all too easy to slip back into his old ways, coming and going in silence.

Long ago he had learned to be prudent with pleasures and frugal with joys. Since his wedding night he had had to practice all the restraint he knew. He had discovered, that first night, that sleeping in his bed without his bride, while she slept in the next room, could not be considered sleeping in the least. He meant only to stay away long enough to check his desire, but that desire was hard to check. To see her was to want her. To be near her was to burn.

One afternoon as he passed the dining room, he had been caught by the sound of her voice. For the longest while he had stood listening to Bel talk to the girl Susan about paint and molding and chair coverings, listening to the little rustle of her skirts and the rise and fall of the fresh, clear voice. That night he had not slept at all.

He looked up from the piece of bread he had crumbled between his fingers to find Farre watching him. Within a day Farre would know exactly how things stood between the master and mistress of Courtland.

"So, lad, it isn't going as well as you hoped," said his friend.

"My hopes were perhaps too high," Nick admitted.

"I doubt it. Seemed a promising match to me."

"Farre, you tried to warn me. I didn't listen then." Nick paused to consider how to word the truth. "I offered her her freedom if she finds she cannot be my wife after all."

There was a brief silence as Farre, who had been pouring another round of home-brewed into the pewter cups, visibly adjusted himself to Nick's admission. "So have you taken her fishing?" he asked.

Nick shook his head.

"Riding?"

"No."

"Walking?"

"Farre . . ." The angry impulse to rebuff his friend's advice died there. "I have not seen her for twelve days."

"That bad, is it? Where have you been sleeping?"

Nick cast an involuntary glance at the bed in the corner of the small room. He planted his elbows on the table and rested his head in his hands. What had seemed a reasonable and decent course of action the morning after their disastrous wedding night now seemed foolish. He would have to face his bride sometime if he wanted her to stay—and he did want her to stay.

"Best go straight to her, lad."

Nick lifted his head. Farre's words echoed his own thoughts. He stood and stared down at his clothes. He had not been to the house all day. His loose white shirt was limp and wrinkled, his corduroy breeches and boots dusty.

"I can't go like this," he complained.

"You thinking I'm your fairy godmother with a wand to wave over you?"

Nick laughed and turned to the door. Just as he reached it, a firm knock sounded against the wood. He pulled it open to discover his bride, her fist raised, her eyes flashing with challenge, her mouth set in a determined line. His laughter died. For a heartbeat or two neither spoke.

Her eyes took in the remains of the simple supper he had shared with Farre, and a look of hurt confusion crossed her face. "You prefer to dine with your groom in the comfort of the stable, rather than eat with your inferior wife at your own table?" she asked.

"You misunderstand," Nick protested, reaching out to hand her over the threshold.

"Oh, I understand all too well," she said, holding her head high and ignoring the offered hand. "You married me to humiliate me, and my family. I congratulate you. You have succeeded very well." As Nick stepped toward her, she spun away, disappearing around the corner of the stable before he could move.

* * *

Bel gripped the limbs of her leafy perch and stared down at the top of her husband's dark head. She held herself very still. She had thought only to distance herself from the scene of her humiliation. She had not anticipated pursuit, and when he had called her name from the fork in the river path, she had taken a child's way out and climbed an old oak that bent toward the Ashe. Below her the river murmured softly. She offered a hasty prayer that her husband would turn away and leave her to nurse her anger alone, but he tilted his head up, and she found herself staring into his very black, suddenly amused eyes.

"Go away," she said. The amusement faded from his eyes, and for a minute she thought he might obey her.

Then he answered. "I have been away." His gaze was solemn but steady. "You wanted to find me."

She didn't deny it and saw a gleam of purpose light his eyes. He scanned her tree, put his foot in the notch that had enabled her to climb it, and began to pull himself up into the branches.

"Surely it's beneath your dignity to climb trees," she suggested.

"I have no dignity where you are concerned," he said. He was quick and strong, and he seemed to have an advanced understanding of the art of tree-climbing. A few swift, easy motions brought him to the long, thick horizontal limb that curved up to her notched perch. He stood there a moment, balanced and grinning in such a way that she feared he meant to walk straight out to her. Then he lowered himself, straddling the branch and leaning back against the great trunk.

"You wanted to say something to me," he said.

She tried for her mother's tone of calm authority, but the sound of his laughter was fresh in her mind, and she thought only of the humiliation her marriage had brought her. "You won't care for what I have to say, my—"

"Nick," he reminded her coolly. "I want to hear every charge you have to bring against me."

"Very well, Nick," she said grimly. "Your whole design has been to humiliate me."

Something like amusement lighted his eyes again. "If I were capable of acting by design in regard to you, believe me, humiliating you would not be my object."

"Then why did you bring your groom and not your family to our wedding?"

It was a direct attack, and she had all the satisfaction of seeing in her husband's eyes that bleak, withdrawn expression that had so startled her as she danced past him at their wedding.

"My family is dead."

"Forgive me—I never thought, I . . ."

"How could you? You have an inexhaustible supply of family."

Bel felt herself stiffen at that, but his next words melted her anger.

"I have Farre."

"An earl—the Earl of Haverly—has no one but his groom?" It was incomprehensible that he had no siblings, no cousins, no aunts or uncles.

"Nick," he corrected automatically. "I meant no insult by bringing Farre."

"But why did you say he was your uncle?" The impertinent question was out before she could stop herself.

He looked away at that and tore a short leafy branch from the limb above him. The river below rushed along with its swift, muted music. He began to strip the leaves from the branch in his hands. She sensed he was remembering things he wished forgotten.

"You are fortunate in your family," he said at length. "You take pride in them and they in you. I wanted somebody—" He paused. "—like that."

And he was telling her, she realized, that he had no one else *like that*. "Have you always known Mr. Farre?" she asked.

He shook his head, but did not raise his eyes to hers. The destruction of the branch in his hands was nearly complete before he spoke again. "I was about your cousin Phillip's age when I was summoned to Haverly. My parents had drowned in an accident the summer before, and my uncle, the earl, decided I would do as an heir. He had a great deal to teach me about the responsibilities I would inherit, and I did not always enjoy the lessons.

"But Uncle Miles was an invalid. He never rode, and I found the stable a safe place to hide. Farre was my uncle's groom. Farre found me in his stable so often he began to teach me things. He taught me to fish, to—"

"You had not fished before?" she asked. She tried to recall the details of the pampered childhood her cousins had invented for him at the wedding. How far from the truth they had been.

He look up and smiled at her. "No. I had learned to climb trees, to read, to swim."

And, she thought, to kiss, a lesson not learned from Farre. And a lesson her husband had learned well. He did not kiss with the awkwardness she remembered in John Lyde or the self-absorbed force of Darlington.

He must have read something of her thoughts in her face, for his hands stopped the restless shredding of the branch and his eyes darkened with that particular intensity that sent a flutter along her nerves. Suddenly the perch she had chosen seemed dizzyingly high. She closed her eyes to steady herself.

When she opened them, he was standing. He extended his right hand and took two sideways steps toward her. "Come," he said, "join me at this end of our bough."

The words were a command, but his voice was coaxing, and she saw in the strong, lean hand reaching out for her an offer of peace. She stretched out her own hand, allowing him to pull her to her feet and lead her to his end of the stout limb. He settled himself against the trunk again, and helped her down to sit before him.

"Lean against me," he urged. This was a different request, and for a moment, she held herself apart from him, but this, too, was a step she must take if she meant to be his wife. Slowly she leaned back, gradually resting her shoulders against his chest, her head against his shoulder. His arms closed around her waist. Through the fine layers of cambric and muslin that separated them, she felt the heat of him and the swift beating of his heart.

"You were right not to insist on our intimacy that first night," she said. She felt him tense at her words, felt his hands tighten briefly at her waist, and hurried to speak her next thought. "But shouldn't we begin to act as husband and wife somewhere?"

She heard his quick indrawn breath.

"Will this tree do?" he asked in a choked voice.

She felt the taut muscle in his arms and the abrupt suspension of his breathing, as if his whole body waited for her answer.

"I confess," she said unsteadily, "I am more conventional in my notions, and thought that we might begin by dining together."

He was silent for some time, and when he spoke again, his voice was even. "Is that what you wanted to complain to me about this evening when you found me with Farre?"

"Among other things. Do you object to husbands and wives dining together?"

"I have not often seen it done, but for your sake I am willing to try it."

His admission startled her and set her wondering again what sort of family his had been. The activities he had described were those of a solitary child. She could not imagine a brother of hers having to escape to the stables to find a friend or a teacher. It was some minutes before she realized that she still leaned against him and the sky had grown dark. She stirred a little, trying to bring herself to a more upright posture.

"Are you afraid to sit so close to me?" he asked.

"Not afraid." She sought the words. "Too conscious of the . . . intimacy, perhaps."

Silence fell between them, filled by the river's constant murmurous tumble down the hillside.

"The day we made our bargain," he said, "I came down to the Ashe after dark and lay on the bank, wishing you beside me like this."

"And since our wedding?" she asked, suspecting from the tone of his revelation that he had made such a wish more than once, unwilling to confess her own reverie of that same evening.

"More than once," he whispered.

She waited then for him to turn her in his arms to ask for one of the bargain kisses, but he remained still and silent and the river rushed by cool and indifferent.

After a time, he suggested, "Let me take you back to the house." He climbed down and helped her after. As soon as they separated she felt all the chill of the damp night air and began to shiver in her thin gown and slippers. He hurried her up the path, surprisingly sure of his way in the darkness.

When they reached the door, he opened it, then caught her in his arms. "Good night," he said. "I will join you for dinner tomorrow."

"You're not coming in?" she asked.

He shook his head. "But I will take a kiss."

"One?" She knew his answer.

"One." He drew her against him with a gentle pull that measured her acquiescence inch by inch until their lips met. At once the kiss deepened, his hunger evoking in her an answering need to give, so that she pressed against him until he wrenched himself from her arms and strode off in the darkness.

"Good night," she whispered.

16

⚜⚜⚜⚜⚜⚜⚜⚜⚜⚜⚜

"THE ROOM IS charming," Nick offered between the first remove and a course of chicken *fricassé* and vegetable pudding. They had passed beyond the weather and the food, and he had been pleased to discover that while he could think only of kisses and kissing, he could still speak on the unobjectionable subject of room decoration.

"Thank you," Bel answered. "You must tell me if there is anything you dislike in the scheme."

Nick looked around, surprised that she could think he wouldn't like her renovation. Pale creamy walls and a handsome red-and-cream stripe on the chairs and hangings had lightened and warmed the room. There was nothing of his uncle's emphasis on display. The watercolors above the mantel and the flowers on the table seemed to soften the room and connect it to the world outside. He met her questioning look.

"There's no clock," she said.

He studied the food on his plate, pushing a piece of chicken through the sauce in a long furrow as he considered his answer. "Would you like a clock?" he asked.

"Would you allow me one?" she countered. "There are no clocks anywhere in this house, except the one my parents gave us, and you had it removed from the hall yesterday."

He saw now how she had taken that act. He had not meant to slight her family. He had thought only to escape the tyranny of time that had ruled his uncle's house. "I apologize for moving the clock without consulting you," he said. "It is a handsome clock, and you may have it placed anywhere you wish." He pushed the bit of chicken into a lump of vegetables.

"In your library?" she asked.

He had to look up, and knew he'd betrayed himself as soon as their eyes met. The faint smile in hers told him she'd deliberately provoked him. He put down his fork and studied her. She was teasing him.

"You could tell me about your objections to clocks ... Nick," she said.

He could, if he could speak. Her voice, low and sweet and hesitating over his name, sent a ripple of heat through him like July sun shimmering over ripening grain. Why had he dressed for dinner with his throat swathed in linen, his limbs confined in layers of wool and silk? She looked so cool in the blue muslin gown that dipped in a lace-edged arc below her slim throat and puffed lightly at her shoulders above bare, rounded arms.

"At Haverly," he began, as much to distract himself as to enlighten his bride, "my uncle had several clocks in each room. He liked to see a clock on every wall, and he insisted that all clocks agree to the minute. I have seen him upbraid a man of his in the severest manner if but one clock in dozens missed the exact chiming of the hour."

Bel wondered what suffering of his own he was concealing. All day she had been thinking over his revelations in the tree, and she guessed that he would always minimize whatever had been difficult or painful for himself.

"How many clocks are there at Haverly?" she asked with careful unconcern.

"Would you believe a thousand?"

A thousand. She made a fleeting attempt to imagine a thousand clocks ticking and chiming, but he was looking at her with undisguised longing, and the image of clocks gave way to an image of the thousand kisses he had once asked for.

"Then let us set our clock awry," she said, striving for a light tone. "Let all the clocks in Courtland ring at twenty minutes past the hour."

"Done," he said, his eyes locked with hers.

It was the first time he had yielded to her. She looked away, unable to answer that gaze with one as frank.

When the footman entered with the next course, she busied herself with the placement of platters. The things about which she and her husband were not speaking possessed her mind, and the little shiver at his nearness started deep in her. She searched for a rational topic of conversation.

"Do you object to any other conventional domestic arrangements?" she asked.

"Neckcloths at dinner on a July evening."

"You prefer to be the shepherd then?"

Again she drew a penetrating look from him, and she realized she had revealed thoughts about him she was not sure she wished to explain. Whatever tale she told him, he was going to know if it was less than the truth.

She felt the heat of a blush rise in her cheeks, but she kept her gaze steady. "When we first met, you stepped out of that wood in a white shirt and corduroy breeches like some character out of a pastoral."

"And do you still see me as such a character?"

"Sometimes I do. You are not at all what I thought you were even two days ago."

She could see she had startled him with her admission, but he did not take his eyes from her. "Should I be glad of that?"

She nodded, unable to speak.

Abruptly he rose and, turning his back to her, strode to the window. There he stood, looking out, his hands braced against the sill. She clasped her own hands in her lap and pressed them together hard to still the trembling. He was going to ask for another of the bargain kisses, and this time she meant to question him about them.

"Would you be willing to ... go fishing?" he asked.

"Fishing? Now?" She turned, astonished, but his back was still to her.

"If we hurry," he said without moving, "we can still catch the evening rise, and ... it will be cool by the river."

She could hardly adjust her thinking to his unexpected invitation. She was so sure she knew that alteration in his eyes that meant he wanted to kiss her. And at least some of the surprise of this moment lay in her recognition that she would be disappointed if he didn't want to. She was staring at his back when he turned.

"Will you come with me?" he asked. The look was still in his eyes.

"Yes," she answered, knowing she had agreed to more than fishing.

Nick sat cross-legged on the rug they had spread above the Ashe and considered the contents of the case Bel had opened before him. Arrayed in precise ordered compartments were dozens of bits of silk, wool, and feathers, cleverly wrapped about sharp barbs to suggest the variety of insect life that hovered above the river during the spring and summer months. Bel was explaining which of these dry flies was apt to be most successful in late July on the Ashe, but the movement of her fingers over the bright lures was distracting.

She had put on a plain brown overdress, concealing one of the light, white muslins she so often wore. She sat beside him, her knee nearly touching his, her movements as she leaned over the box of lures bringing sweet hints of lavender and woman to his eager senses. He was tempted to curse the widow who had taught him nearly every degree of rising desire. He could not pretend to himself that he did not recognize the danger of indulging in this quiet closeness. Abruptly he asked Bel for a lure.

She broke off her sentence and looked at him questioningly, and he met her gaze, letting her see the desire that consumed him. If she chose to back away from him now, to end their expedition, he would understand. But she nodded and looked down at the lures. She selected one and looked up again, offering it to him. When his fingers brushed her palm as he took the offered fly, she did not flinch.

Bel watched her husband attach the lure to his line, then spring to his feet in one fluid motion and move to the edge of the river, positioning himself with care to take advantage of an opening in the trees that made for easy casting. She watched with entire approval the precise rhythm of each cast that sent the fly, leader, and line descending as lightly as a breeze-borne leaf to the river below. It was satisfying to see that she had married a man whose fishing she would not blush for among the Shaws, but it was another sort of feeling altogether to watch the hasty way he was setting the hook. He was too fast, and though the trout were biting, he was losing them from impatience or distraction. She drew up her knees, hugging them as if she could steady the slight trembling of her limbs, closing her eyes and concentrating on the sweet, playful music of the river. A moment later her husband gave an exclamation of disgust, and she heard him climb back up the bank to their rug. She looked up.

"Your turn," he said. He stripped his line, separated the segments of the pole, and lowered himself to a place beside her again.

She selected a tiny, shimmering green imitation of a shell fly, attached it to her leader, and rose, wondering if her concentration would prove any better than his. "Wish me luck," she urged.

"Good luck," he said.

Nick knew at once that watching Bel fish his river was just the sort of pleasure that he could come to crave unreasonably. She chose a spot where shadow and light mixed. In her brown dress she looked like a woodland nymph. Her bright hair wanted only a crown of ivy leaves to complete the image. It was an unfortunate image, for it made him think of Daphne fleeing Apollo's kiss, but Bel had not fled, nor had she questioned him about his determination to hold her to their bargain.

For the first time he saw the flimsiness of their bargain now that they had married. Only her honor and his desire held it together, for, in truth, he would not expose her brothers if she refused him. And he should free her.

He could see the truth of her uncle's story about her fishing prowess in each cast. She was sure and graceful and willing to cast to the places trout liked best, the osier-fringed bank or the deep narrow slot where water spilling down from the rocks above brought the trout their food. On the fourth or fifth cast—he'd lost count—she got a bite, and with a deft pull on her line, she set the barbed hook in the trout's mouth. Nick was on his feet in an instant, at her side in two.

"Did you see him?" she asked, without turning. The trout arched from the water in a silvery flash, twisting desperately to dislodge the hook.

"Easily three pounds," said Nick. He grabbed their net and prepared to help her, admiring the combination of will and cunning with which she worked the pole and line, drawing the fish ever closer to the shore. When she had coaxed her catch into the shallows, Nick waded into the river and wielded their net. A quick blow finished it. He cut the line and held her prize up for her admiration. She smiled at him with open delight, and the pleasure in her look sent a surge of warmth through him even as he stood in the cool waters of the Ashe.

"Shall we have this beauty *poached* for dinner tomorrow?" he asked.

"Aunt Margaret's recipe?" she countered, laughing.

She looked then like some bright white blossom discovered along a wooded path, but he couldn't tell her that. "I want a kiss," he said.

"Here?" Her glance took in the distance between them, his boots planted in the river, and the netted trout hanging from his hand.

He lifted his gaze from hers and looked up the bank to their rug spread among ferns, and an image from his dreams came back to him. "Will you lie with me on the rug?" he asked. Two bright spots of color flamed in her cheeks, and he cursed himself for the clumsiness of his phrasing. "Just for this kiss," he assured her.

Bel could not speak to his suggestion immediately. Her throat was suddenly dry and her pulse pounding. "Can we talk first?" she asked. The question made him look doubtful, but he nodded and stepped out of the stream.

They mounted the bank together, and while she knelt to put away her fishing gear, he carefully packed her catch in their basket. He made one more trip to the river, dipping his hands in the water, washing away the scent and scales of the trout.

She sat, her hands clasped in her lap. He returned, cast her a quick glance, then stretched out beside her on the rug, his face lifted to the evening sky, his eyes closed. It was not going to be easy to ask him what she meant to ask.

"How many kisses do I owe you?"

His eyes did not open, but a flicker of pain crossed his face. "Do you consider the kiss in the church one of the bargain kisses?" he asked.

"No," she said softly. It would be unjust of her to treat that kiss, required by their circumstances, as one of the kisses she had agreed to give for her brothers' safety.

"Seven."

His answer was so definite, so unhesitating, it sent a tremor through her. *Seven*—not so many after all. Seven kisses could burn away in an hour or a few minutes, perhaps, unless one . . . She looked at the reclining shepherd beside her and thought of pleasures she had hoarded in lonely times. Letters from Tom deliberately kept in a pocket all day, so that she might savor the anticipated news. Books closed, their endings delayed so that she might remain lost in the fiction. She understood now why he asked for just one kiss at a time.

As if he sensed her gaze on him, his eyes opened, dark and hungry. "Are you still willing to give me a kiss?" he asked.

She nodded.

He rolled toward her, propping his head in his hand as he leaned on one elbow. With his other hand he drew her down to lie facing him. Then his arm encircled her waist, and he pulled her against him. As their bodies came together, she raised her hand and pushed against his chest. "Wait," she urged him.

He tipped back his head, drawing a deep shaky breath, and she could not help moving her hand a little across the smooth, firm contours of his chest. Beneath her palm his heart pounded wildly. Her hand trembled.

"What?" he demanded hoarsely.

"Whatever happens now," she said, "promise me you won't . . . stay away again. You'll come to dinner at night."

He swallowed and nodded and drew her closer. His hand slid up her back and tangled in her hair, pulling her head forward until their lips met. And she discovered that a kiss was not after all a single emotion transmuted into touch, but a play of feelings, as many-noted as the river winding through the darkening wood.

For the first time she felt the deeper note of longing in his kiss and strove to answer it. She touched his cheek and felt him pause. Then with a sudden fierce energy he broke the kiss and rolled her onto her back, covering her body with his own. One hand still cupped her head. His other hand came up to stroke her throat, the palm resting against her collarbone. Her hand fell away from his cheek.

For a moment the longing in his dark eyes was plain, as it had been in the church. Then his mouth descended to hers again, and his taut, lean frame pressed urgently against her. For a moment her body strained upward in answer to his, and where their bodies met at the juncture of hip and thigh, he rocked against her once. She stilled, recognizing where this advance in their intimacy must lead, and he shuddered and slid from her to lie on their rug, his face cradled in his hands, his breathing harsh and unsteady.

"Forgive . . . me," he said. "That . . . was not . . . our bargain."

Bel pushed herself up. She did not trust herself to speak or stand. Her pulse raced, and her limbs shook with an unreleased tension. She crossed her arms before her and clasped her elbows tightly, drawing a steadying breath. She did like her husband's kisses, kisses that had the power to make her forget their bargain and the circumstances of their marriage and the insults to her family that still divided them and must keep her from his bed.

He looked so very unhappy she reached out and touched his shoulder, but he shook her off.

"Don't . . . touch me . . . now," he warned. "Go in. Go in, if you want me to keep my promise."

She rose then, looking about her a little blindly, and stumbled to the edge of the path. Looking down, she reminded him, "You promised you would not stay away."

He nodded but did not lift his head.

The stable smelled of hay as fresh and sweet as hope. The brisk rhythms of currying brushes, chaff-cutters, and brooms, accompanied by a low mumbling sort of chatter among the stable boys, greeted Bel as she entered.

"Good morning," she called out.

Farre appeared at the entrance to one of the stalls and nodded to her. "Good morning, my lady," he said. "Would you like a horse readied?"

"No, thank you, Mr. Farre," she answered. "Is . . . is my husband about?"

"Haven't seen the l—his lordship yet today, my lady."

"You don't call him that, do you, Mr. Farre?"

"Only to anger him."

Bel digested that. The man knew her husband perhaps better than anyone. Farre turned back to the mare he was grooming and led the horse out into the aisle between the banks of stalls.

"You've known my husband since he was a . . . boy?" she asked.

"Since he came to Haverly." Farre inspected the horse's feet. Then he retrieved a bit, bridle, and saddle from the tack room. He slipped the bit and bridle on the horse. The little mare tossed her head once, and Bel stepped up to stroke the velvety nose.

"Is Haverly very grand?"

"Very." Farre flung the saddle on the horse's back.

"I suppose there is a great ballroom there."

"Aye." Farre bent down to adjust the cinch.

"And the society there is very fine?"

"There's no society there." Farre straightened and tested the saddle's fit.

"No society? But who comes to the dinners and balls?"

"The old earl gave no dinners, nor balls. He couldn't abide 'em, didn't like ladies."

"And my hus—Nick, did he give balls?" She had to ask.

"Never."

"Why did he buy Courtland? For the river?"

"Aye, and to have something of his own." Farre looked at her, apparently assessing her reaction to his words.

When Bel let her doubts on that point show, he continued. "Nothing at Haverly belonged to . . . his lordship, my lady."

"You mean 'Nick.' But it must all belong to him now," she protested.

Farre snorted. "As long as he leaves everything just the way it is. A museum it is."

"Even the clocks?" Bel asked.

Farre looked at her sharply. "Especially the clocks." Then he smiled, and suddenly Bel felt she had a friend. She smiled back.

"You're sure you won't ride, my lady?" he asked.

"No, thank you, Mr. Farre, and I don't want to be called 'my lady.' 'Bel' will do." She turned to go.

"Are you off to the river, then?"

She nodded.

"Aye, I thought so."

It was Auggie's voice she heard first, clear and distinct above the rush of water. "I don't like it."

"You don't have a better idea, Shaw," came Darlington's voice in reply.

"What are you two doing here?" Bel asked, coming into the open along the bank above the spot where she and Nick had fished the night before. Darlington was kneeling at the edge of the river, an open basket at his side, a vial in his hand. Auggie looked up, glanced quickly at his companion, and shifted his stance so that he blocked her view of the kneeling man.

"We came to fish, of course," Auggie said. She frowned at him. "It's true," he went on. "The earl gave all the Shaws permission to fish his spots."

"When?" she asked.

"Just as soon as the honeymoon was over," replied Auggie. There was a smugness in his tone that Bel found most annoying.

"The honeymoon *is* over, isn't it, Bel?" mocked Darlington, rising.

"Hardly," she said, but she could not speak with quite the assurance she wished to have.

"Or did it ever begin?" he taunted her. "Where's your bridegroom, Bel? Does he have pressing business at the far end of Courtland again today?"

"You shouldn't have married him, Bel," put in Auggie.

"Auggie Shaw, you have no right to say such things."

"Oh, don't I? Well, it's just what Tom would say. Why didn't you wait for Tom to be there? You think I don't know it was a havey-cavey affair?"

"Havey-cavey affair!" She spoke as forcefully as she could, but Auggie's mention of not waiting for Tom hurt. She turned to Darlington. "Mr. Darlington, what have you been suggesting to my brother about my marriage?"

Darlington shrugged. "What is there to suggest, Bel?"

Bel forced herself to speak calmly. "Auggie, if there was any unseemly haste in our marrying, you may blame your friend Darlington, who forced us to announce our betrothal before we . . . were ready."

"Well, Darlington didn't force you to kiss the earl in the squire's garden."

No, you did, she thought. *To save you I made a bargain. And here you are at the river again, up to no good.* She glanced at the basket at Darlington's feet. It was closed. There were no rods or nets anywhere, and Auggie had not brought the dog. "Why are you here, Auggie?" she asked.

Nick had left his room before dawn, intending to so occupy his time and his thoughts that there would be no room for images of lying with Bel, but when he had returned from his morning ride, the stable hand who had taken his horse volunteered the information that he had just missed her ladyship. The further information that she had taken the river path led him to turn his steps in that direction. She could not entirely resent his passion of the night before if she was willing to return to the scene of their lovemaking. When he came to the end of the path, however, he was forced to change his mind about his bride's motives. It seemed she had gone to the river to meet her brother and her former suitor.

"Don't be hard on the boy, Bel," Nick heard Darlington say, "just because he sees through your sham marriage."

Nick could not hear Bel's reply over the pounding of his own heart.

"I think I *must* speak, Bel," Darlington said, "when your family isn't here to speak, when you've ignored their invitations for a sennight, when your husband is seen everywhere without you . . ."

"You aren't even part of the family anymore." It

was Auggie Shaw's voice. Nick drew nearer, letting the trees conceal him.

"Of course I am," came Bel's voice, clear now that Nick had taken a position just above the speakers. "There is nothing I care more for than my family. Even through this marriage, for which you blame me, I will be doing things for all of you. But you must not let the earl find you here without your fishing gear, Auggie."

"He hasn't yet," said Auggie. Darlington laughed. "I hope he never does," came Bel's reply.

Nick did not hear the next remarks clearly. Darlington and the boy seemed to be gathering up some things at the river's edge. Then Bel and her companions moved off down the path along the bank, and he was left with his thoughts.

He stepped out of the trees and descended to the river, blue in the sunlight against the green of the reeds, clear in the shadows before him. He had been unguarded with Bel, letting the mask of their bargain slip, revealing his feelings for her while she remained indifferent to him. He should have known better. His parents had had their lovers, his uncle had had his possessions, and Bel *Shaw* had had her family. If no one particularly needed or wanted him, so be it. He would have his river. A trout broke the surface where insect wings caught the sunlight. Flopping back in the water, it scattered sparkling drops. The trouble was, Nick did not think he could look at that sparkle without wanting Bel.

By Bel's count, Gerry, their young footman, had now contributed three more words to the dinner conversation than Nick had. She stole a glance at him. His face was set in rigid, haughty lines; his eyes were cold, his neck swathed in yards of crisp linen. She had a vivid recollection of the evening before, when he lay beside her, his head thrown back, his throat bare and taut with emotion. Then she had been touching him; now he seemed unreachable.

But he had come to dinner. Whatever had happened to make the passionate shepherd of the night before appear so cold and distant now, he had not forgotten his promise to dine with her. And she must do what she could to bring her husband and her family together. So when Gerry left them to their dessert, she summoned her courage and mentioned that Richard and Mary were giving a farewell dinner for her London cousins.

"If you wish to attend, by all means do so," he said with cold civility.

"I wish to go with you."

"Why?" he asked, giving his attention to a thin slice of cheese on his plate.

"We did not begin our marriage well, but I think we have done better these past two days, and we might do better still if we appeared together as husband and wife."

He lifted angry eyes to hers. "But we are husband and wife in name only. Did you wish it to be otherwise?"

"There are still obstacles to our . . . union," she said, thinking of Auggie and the sadness she felt at seeing him under Darlington's influence.

"Dozens of them."

"You mean my family, I suppose, but you must—"

"Neither you nor your family has any use for me except to provide a river and pin money, and I can do both without attending any Shaw dinners." He stood and tossed his napkin on the table. "You go. We have only a *sham* marriage, and I am no good at pretending. Excuse me." He bowed and walked out.

Bel picked up the little box she had concealed beside the flowers on her side of the table and lifted the lid. Inside were three flies she had tied for him that afternoon. Though she had not seen him all day, she

had imagined they would talk and laugh and stroll
to the river. With the sweetness of their kisses still in
her mind, it had been easy to imagine his saying yes
to a Shaw dinner. She had gone so far as to imagine
dancing with him in Richard and Mary's parlor. At
least there had been no witnesses to her humiliation.

Nick leaned against the windowsill, staring at the
moon-brightened landscape. A nightingale sang in
the wood and, nearer, insects hummed. He had
avoided his bed for hours now, but he felt the emp-
tiness of it, of the room behind him, while the night
beyond his window seemed to pulse with life. What
he wanted was tantalizingly close, in the next room.
He felt a bit like Tantalus, standing in his particular
pool in hell, reaching for the sweet fruit that would
ease his hunger, and having it withdrawn even as his
fingers seemed about to clasp it.

When had desire sharpened into this longing for
one girl? After years of comfortable indifference to
his parents' indiscreet couplings, he had been awakened to his own lust by the widow who had been
stranded in the Seymour household the summer he
was fifteen. What she had stirred in him had been
lulled to sleep by the dreary routine of his uncle's
rigid establishment. But the parade of temptresses in
town had roused the sleeping beast with a fury.
Dreams of breasts and thighs and hands reaching for
his aching body had disturbed his rest and sent him
fleeing to Courtland. There, in one moment, a girl
standing in a steam, lost in admiration for the shining beauty of the river, had begun to sharpen all his
desire to this keen edge that seemed to pierce his
heart more each day.

Earlier, riding about Courtland after he had
stormed out of the dining room, he had indulged
himself imagining he might have avoided his desire
for Bel. What if he had allowed himself to be fully se-

duced by the widow? What if he had assuaged his lust with one of the beauties of London? But he knew that thinking was false and he understood why, even before he met Bel, he had been unwilling to seek those comforts. His parents' energetic couplings had not been unions at all. He himself had never felt more lonely, more isolated, than he had in the bed of the woman who had stirred him at fifteen. Now, if he gave in to his desire for Bel before he won her love, that would be empty too. And to win her love, he was going to have to humble himself. He was going to have to accept that he meant less to her than her family. He was going to have to go to that dinner.

From next door came the scrape of the window being pushed open. Nick's heart hammered in response. He crossed to the connecting door between the two rooms and knocked.

Silence.

"Bel, are you awake?" he asked. "Can I speak with you?"

After a minute he heard the key turn in the lock. The door opened. Moonlight streamed in from the open window. Bel stood before him in a white gown, her hair silver in the white light, her eyes wide.

"I was angry and rude at dinner. I apologize," he said. He made no move to enter the room.

"I forgive you," she answered.

"I would like to go to the dinner with you."

"I'm glad." She smiled. "Come in?"

"I think not," he said, but he couldn't take his eyes off her.

"The moon is beautiful," she offered.

"Yes, were you looking at it from your window?"

"Yes, were you?"

"Yes." His whole body strained to move toward her and take her in his embrace. Carefully, he put a hand on the door frame and gripped it firmly.

"I don't suppose you are ready to come to my bed yet?" he found himself asking.

"No," she said, taking a step back.

He nodded and looked over his shoulder at his room. He should step back too, end the conversation—now.

"Wait," she said. She crossed the room, away from the moonlight, a white blur in the shadows, and returned with a box. She held it out to him, and he pulled his fingers loose from the door frame to reach for her gift.

"I tied these for you today," she said.

"Today? When?" he asked, lifting the lid on the little box.

"This afternoon. Why?"

"I did not think you liked me this afternoon."

"I do like you." She hesitated. "I want you to like . . . my family, and I want them to like you."

"I like the dog," he said. It was true—and more than he could yet say for the others.

"You are teasing," she said. "I like you to tease."

"I like it, too," he said with some difficulty as a particularly hot wave of desire crested in him. "I should go."

"I know," she said, as if she recognized the thing he was struggling with. "It's just that we are talking, not arguing, and it is nice and . . ."

"Will you come with me to the river in the morning?"

"I will."

"Shut the door and lock it," he said. "Good night."

"Good night."

He stepped back, allowing her to close the door, and listened for the scrape of the key in the lock. When he heard it, he turned and crossed to his bedside. With shaking hands he fumbled for the tinderbox and lit a candle. He pulled his Scott novel from under a pillow and resolutely set himself to read.

17

An overcast morning gave the river a dull pewter look, and Bel and Nick argued about how best to describe rain from a trout's point of view as they made their way down the hill through the woods.

Then they reached the bank above the pool. Six dead trout floated on the surface, drifting like logs, all the liquid silver movement of the living fish stilled—pale bellies up, fixed mouths gaping, no flutter of gills or tails.

"No," Bel cried.

Nick swore. He scanned the opposite bank and then began to examine the ground where they stood. Bel sank onto a rock and stared at the ugly sight in the pool. But in her mind she saw Darlington bending down at the water's edge with something in his hand, something that Auggie had not wanted her to see. When Nick looked at her, she lowered her gaze.

"There's nothing here to suggest who did this," he said quietly. "But you know, don't you?"

She looked up. His eyes were unreadable. "I do not *know*, but I would like to question . . . someone about it."

He nodded and turned away. "Let's go back," he said. "I want to get Farre. These fish have to be removed."

"I'll help," she said, wanting to show him that she was on his side in this matter.

"No. I don't want you near the water." He whirled and faced her, his dark eyes burning. His curt refusal of her help stung her. This river that they both loved seemed destined to divide them.

He must have read her expression, for he spoke again more gently. "First we need to know whether the river is poisoned or merely the fish." He held out a hand to help her up.

She took his hand and rose. He looked once more at the spoiled pool and then drew her with him up the path, his stride purposeful and swift, his anger just barely controlled.

Halfway up the path she pulled against the hand that held hers, and stopped, bracing herself against his momentum. He halted and turned to face her. She drew a steadying breath.

"I know you are angry, and justly so, but will you still come with me tonight to Richard and Mary's?"

His eyes searched hers, then fell to their clasped hands. "I will," he said.

The trees outside Mary Shaw's drawing-room window bent low and sprang abruptly upright with the gusting wind. Rain drummed intermittently against the panes. But the fire in the hearth flared brightly and the logs popped as Mary led her female guests in from the dining room. Bel refused to take precedence over her sister-in-law at a family dinner, so she entered with her cousins.

"Bel, your husband is just as dull as all the men hereabouts," complained Ellen. "He hardly talked of anything but the Hilcombe trial."

"I could forgive him that," said Fanny, "but he asked Richard about Talavera, and you know how often we have had to endure that story."

Louisa laughed. "The worst was talking about the harvest. 'Will the rain spoil the crops?' "

"Is your earl so dull at home, Bel?" asked Fanny.

"Never!" she said. At her passionate, unhesitating defense of him everyone turned to stare. And she blushed, conscious of the false picture of their marriage they had been presenting all evening. But Nick must not be judged harshly by them. The Shaws must see past the fine clothes and stiff demeanor her husband adopted in company.

She was grateful when Mary called the ladies' attention to the wild flailing of the trees outside the window, but it was not a view that could hold Ellen, Louisa, and Fanny long, and even Bel's aunts and Mrs. Darlington soon turned away, drawn to the warmth of the fire. Bel lingered with her mother and Mary.

"It's so wild a storm for this time of year," said Mary. "Does it mean anything, do you think?" She was looking at Serena with particular interest, so Bel left them to their conversation.

She seated herself at the pianoforte and resolutely set herself to play a lively tune. Storms always made her wonder where Tom was, but tonight she found her attention wandering to her husband in the dining room next door, face-to-face with Alan Darlington and surrounded by the Shaw men.

Nick had been reluctant at best to keep their engagement for the evening, and until he knocked at her door, she had doubted he would come. In their carriage he had explained that poisoned bait had been fed to the trout; nothing had been added directly to the water. He had said little else except to ask her to remind him who was who among her relatives. Then he had listened with solemn attention to her recital of names and connections while the little flutter of awareness spread outward along her nerves until she was trembling. "You're cold," he had said, and she had let him think so.

Her mother and Mary strolled from the window to

the fire arm in arm, looking pleased with one another, and Bel stopped playing.

· "Mary has some wonderful news," Serena announced. She stepped back and let her quiet daughter-in-law speak.

"Richard and I are to have another child in April," said Mary.

There were so many exclamations and questions that everyone seemed to be talking at once; Mary beamed, trying to answer them all. Bel left the pianoforte to offer her best wishes to her sister-in-law, and the thought struck her that she herself might have such an announcement to make if she were sharing her husband's bed. To think of it made her warm, though she was far from the fire. But to do it she would have to say she wanted such intimacy between them.

"At least Princess Charlotte has made the tiresome thing fashionable," said Fanny.

"Oh, Fanny, do let Mary enjoy her moment," said Bel.

"When will you have an announcement, Bel?" asked Louisa sharply. The question drew the eyes of her aunts and Mrs. Darlington. Bel felt the heat rise in her cheeks but tipped her chin up defiantly.

"Why, when it's my turn, Louisa," she said.

Then the men entered, and it was plain that Richard had announced the coming birth to them. Bel's father came forward at once to take Mary's hands and tell her how pleased he was to hear of yet another grandchild coming into the world.

Bel looked for Nick and found him listening, with every appearance of polite attention, to something Uncle Charles was saying. She could not help but stare, and, as if he felt her gaze, he glanced at her— and slowly, wondrously, he grinned. It was one of those rare unguarded moments when he let her see the warm feeling in those near-black eyes of his. She

had the distinct impression that her husband had
had his share of the port. She sought to hide her response to that glowing look by returning to the pianoforte and leafing through the music.

It was Darlington, not her husband, who joined
her there almost at once.

"Are you going to play a reel for us, Bel?" he
asked.

"I might, if there's a request for dancing," she said
with cool civility, wondering how to get the truth out
of Darlington about the poisoned fish.

"And will you dance?"

"If I am not needed at the instrument," she replied.

"Will your husband dance?"

Bel studied the music sheets before her. It was a
question she could not answer with any certainty.

"It won't do, Bel. You can't convince me you and
your earl have got a real marriage," Darlington said.

"Mr. Darlington," Bel replied, speaking in a low,
taut voice, "my marriage is not a subject I will discuss with you. What I wish to hear from you is what
you and my brother were doing along the Ashe yesterday when I came upon you."

"Auggie told you—fishing." Darlington placed a
hand on the instrument and was leaning negligently
against it, but he was not meeting her gaze.

"With poisoned bait?" she asked.

His eyes betrayed him with a sudden quick glance
at her.

"It was an ugly act," she said.

"If I am guilty of it, so is your brother," he said,
leaning intimately toward her.

Bel looked at Nick and found his eyes fixed on her.
Darlington caught the look and laughed with such
smug assurance that she longed to slap his arrogant
face.

"You'll never tell your titled husband your brother's crimes, Bel." He bowed a mocking bow and

strolled over to the table where the tea service had been set out and Mary had begun to pour.

Darlington was right about the dilemma she faced. If things were better between Nick and herself, she might have told him about Auggie. If Auggie had not hurt the Ashe, things might have been better between Bel and Nick. She looked at Nick, but he turned away and strolled to the window to gaze out at the storm. He seemed as distant as ever.

Though he had heard every word of Charles Shaw's explanation of how a postponement of the Hilcombe trial had been managed, Nick had been watching Darlington talk to Bel. He was so incensed by the manner in which the big man leaned over the pianoforte toward his wife that he found it necessary to stroll to the dark, cool windows beyond which the storm lashed the trees. He was conscious, too, of having consumed more wine than he usually allowed himself. The effect was not entirely unpleasant. Whenever his eyes met Bel's, he felt a surge of desire course through him unchecked. He had been most careful to keep a close guard on his tongue at those moments. In truth, he was not sure he could speak with his senses so full of his wife's mere presence in the room. He had barely steadied himself when Darlington appeared at his side. The man blocked Nick's view of the others. Nick gauged his adversary's stance warily.

"So, Haverly," Darlington began, "how's your Courtland property doing?"

"Fine," said Nick. He stared out the window at the storm.

"You certainly have been the attentive landlord this past fortnight. Your tenants sing your praises in the public room."

The tone made Nick tense his muscles and shift his

stance, anticipating an attack, but he answered mildly. "I am gratified to serve them well."

"And do you serve your *wife* well?" Darlington asked.

Nick whirled to face the other man and with the sudden movement felt the alcohol swirl like a mist in his brain. His fists clenched, and only Farre's training kept him from throwing a wild first punch. Judgment prevailed. The eyes of others in the room were on them. *Damn.* He could not fight the man here, now.

"You choose well in making your insults in the safety of this drawing room, Darlington," he said quietly. "Don't make them anywhere else. I have the right to defend Bel now."

"I can say what I want anywhere and everywhere in Ashecombe. Bel was meant for me, and I'll have her yet."

Nick knew a flash of self-doubt, but he kept his gaze steady. Bel might not truly be his, but that she was meant for Darlington he couldn't credit. He let his fists open. If Uncle Miles had taught him anything, it was the power of a cutting word.

"By whom was she meant for you? By your own arrogant designation?" Nick had the satisfaction of seeing Darlington flush.

"By her family. Look about you, Haverly. I've known these people all my life, and I know Bel. She's too proud to have a husband who will look down on her family."

"It is fortunate, then, that she married me rather than you, Darlington, for you have a habit of showing contempt for her and all the Shaws. Excuse me."

Nick gave a sudden glance over Darlington's left shoulder, then stepped right, neatly eluding his adversary. He sauntered to the tea table, accepted a cup of coffee from Mary Shaw, and turned toward the pianoforte. He raised the cup to his lips, letting his pulse slow even as he considered Darlington as an opponent. It was plain from the style of the man's verbal attack that with his size Darlington had never felt obliged to learn strategy. Darlington would put all his energy into the first punches, confident he could stun opponents with one or two blows. Lord, it would be sweet to plant the man a facer.

Nick was roused from this satisfying reverie by a sudden stir in the room. Darlington had left his awkward position by the windows and joined Bel's cousins in a knot around the instrument. Ellen Fletcher emerged from the group and hurried from Mary to Richard Shaw, and suddenly she was approaching him.

"We're to have dancing, your lordship. Will you join us?" She didn't wait for an answer but skipped away to speak to her mother and aunts. Nick looked for Bel, but she was surrounded by cousins. He lowered his cup to the saucer and laid the china aside on a nearby table. The self-satisfied glow of his encounter with Darlington faded. He was sure to make a fool of himself in front of Bel now.

"Haverly, will you help us move a few things?" asked Mr. Fletcher.

Nick nodded.

When Ellen, bored with talk of babies and storms, proposed dancing, Darlington immediately agreed. Bel looked for Nick. His back was to her as he accepted a cup of coffee from Mary. His refusal to dance at their wedding had been one of the most hurtful things he had done to her, and she had no doubt that Darlington's enthusiastic support of Ellen's suggestion was meant to test Nick. Surely he would dance with her now, and surely a waltz in the drawing room would lead to a kiss in the carriage.

For a few minutes there was a great deal of confusion as sofas, tables, and chairs were carried to the edges of the room. Then a footman was sent for and the rug rolled up. Mary volunteered to play for them first, and the only thing remaining to be resolved was whether to begin with a country dance or a quadrille.

At that moment Ellen turned to Nick. "Let Lord Haverly decide," she urged.

Bel looked at her husband. He seemed stunned. Everyone was watching. Nick looked down as if considering the question seriously. When he looked up, he gave Bel a brief rueful smile. Then he assumed his gravest expression.

"Miss Fletcher," he said to Ellen, "I am not the one to advise this company in the matter of dancing. My Uncle Miles believed that dancing was the chief accomplishment of savages and never allowed it at Haverly." He glanced at Bel, and this time she saw a reckless gleam in his eye. "I don't know how to dance."

The silence was as complete as if he'd announced he had a third arm.

Then Augustus stepped forward and put his arm about Nick's shoulder. "Son," he said, "you have come to the right place. Bel, I trust you are willing to teach his lordship a step or two? Mary, let us have a quadrille."

They formed three squares with Darlington and Phillip partnering Ellen and Louisa, Nick and Bel paired with Richard and Fanny, and Augustus and Serena paired with Aunt and Uncle Fletcher. It was Darlington who insisted they begin with a most intricate variation of the dance, a suggestion met by giggles from his partner. Bel looked at Nick, who shrugged, as if to say he was game for anything.

After walking through the sequence once, they allowed Mary to play. Bel was not surprised at her husband's quick grasp of the pattern of the dance, but his ease of movement, an ease she had observed often enough in other settings, astonished her. The stiff manner with which he usually held himself in company seemed to dissolve under the influence of the music.

Though Darlington must be accounted the more accomplished dancer, and Bel felt he wanted her to notice his skill, Nick entered the dancing with a wholeheartedness that more than made up for his occasional missteps. And with all the occasions for touching his hand and meeting his eye that the dance afforded, it was she who was breathless in the end. Still she would have gladly begun to waltz, but at a lull in the storm outside her father called an end to the evening.

Wine was poured all around and the departing London Shaws, the baby-to-be, and the newlyweds were toasted. Then Bel's father asked to say one more thing. He drew Serena to his side and announced, "Some time ago, from a gathering such as this, we sent Tom off to the navy. In a fortnight he will be returning to us—a captain."

It was a signal for a great deal of noise and confusion. Everyone embraced everyone. Phil let out a series of "hurrahs." Ellen laughed, and Darlington whirled her about the room in a mad waltz. Aunt Margaret declared that she must make custard, and Fanny and Louisa complained of the injustice of Tom's returning just after their own visit ended. Bel turned from her parents' embraces to find her husband standing quietly in the midst of these joyful effusions.

His expression was somber, but he took her hand and gave it a squeeze. "Your brother must be some fellow to inspire so much . . . joy. I look forward to meeting him."

Bel did not know what she answered. Tom would not be looking forward to meeting Nick. Tom would be thinking only of her letters, letters that portrayed Nick as her enemy. She had not written since . . . since her marriage. Tom had received only her first impressions of her husband, not her later, more informed opinions. And in those letters she had delighted in representing Nick in the worst possible light. It had been a satisfying exercise of her wit to paint him in the blackest colors.

At the time she had not been conscious of doing him an injury. She had believed herself the injured party. Now she saw how unwilling she had been to consider his point of view. Nick had once accused her family of self-importance, and she saw how right he was. Her shepherd was far more humble than her proud relations.

18

NICK SLOWED HIS steps. At the door to Bel's bedroom just a few feet away, their brief show of being the happy bride and groom would end. She walked beside him without speaking, her golden head bent, drops of rain sparkling in her hair. She smelled of the cool rain, woodbine, and her sweet self, and Nick had no wish to relinquish even the light touch of her hand on his arm. But he would. During the carriage ride home he had resolved to return to Haverly for a time.

He had been so sure that insisting upon Bel's marriage to him was right. But tonight he had seen all his reasoning as false. The protection of his name and the advantages of his wealth were paltry compared with the riches of the Shaws.

For a few brief hours he, Nick, had been admitted to their company as if he were one of them, but perhaps the wine had misled him on that point. He had faced Darlington on the strength of that feeling of acceptance. Then he had seen joy transform the faces of the Shaws at the announcement of Tom Shaw's impending return. It would be something to matter like that to a family like the Shaws. Nick would not forget his wife's face under the first influence of the happy news. Nor could he forget how suddenly stricken she had appeared when she turned to him, as if her connection to him had diminished her connection to those she loved.

All the elation he had felt while dancing with her left him then. Amid the family's plans for a grand welcoming dinner, Nick and Bel had taken a quiet leave. In the carriage neither had spoken, and other points of the evening had come back to haunt Nick. The long discussions of the Hilcombe trial had shown him how susceptible Bel had been to his bargain. He had been prepared to accuse her brothers of the very sort of destructive violence for which the Hilcombe villagers might be condemned. But he had not meant their sweet bargain to go so far. He had bargained for kisses, and those kisses had cost Bel far more than he had meant them to, more than he had realized when he insisted on their marriage.

He had claimed to free her on their wedding night, but she was not free while he still insisted on those kisses. Apart from her, at Haverly, perhaps he could gain the strength to free her entirely.

They stopped at her door, and she slipped her hand from his arm and turned to face him. She clasped her hands together as if to steady herself for a speech. But whatever she meant to say went unsaid, and she looked away.

"I am going to leave for Haverly tomorrow morning," he told her.

She lifted a troubled gaze to his at once.

"It's ... business," he said, "and I will be back before your brother arrives."

She looked away again.

"I take back half of what I've said about your family," he offered.

"Half?" She looked up, a faint smile in her eyes.

"Maybe after another party, I will take back the rest," he said lightly.

She nodded. There was a little silence between them. She seemed to study him, and he closed and unclosed his fists, determined to refrain from touching her.

"I'm glad you told us about the dancing," she said at last.

"I am too," he confessed. "I enjoyed dancing with you."

"Will you . . . dance again?"

The question surprised him, but the answer was easy. "Yes." He took a step back. Suddenly it was impossible to linger at her door and not touch her.

"Good night," he whispered. "If I do not see you in the morning—good-bye."

"Good night," she said.

He began to back away. Then, with more resolution than he believed he possessed, he turned and strode rapidly down the hall.

"Wait," she called softly. "Where are you going?"

"I'll be in the library." *Anywhere but in the room next to hers.*

She gave him a doubtful look.

"Don't worry about me. Good night."

Bel stood in a wan patch of light at the entrance to the stable, fighting the strange hollow feeling that had possessed her ever since her husband left. She drew her shawl about her in the cool morning air. It was not quite sunrise, and yet she'd left her bed compelled by a restlessness she could not overcome.

She had lain awake many nights since he left, wondering at his reasons for going. It was silly to think he had left her for other than business reasons. After all, large properties such as he possessed could not manage themselves. But she was painfully aware that just when she had come to like the bargain kisses, he had stopped asking for them. And, equally troubling to her sleep, was the matter of her failure to confess her letters to Tom. At her door that evening Nick had been looking at her with admiration and desire, and she had not wished to trade those looks for looks of anger.

It seemed that every time she and Nick reached some small accord, her family came between them. They could hardly have the proper regard and esteem for one another that a husband and wife should have if she could not tell him the truth. But he could hardly respect and love a woman who had so unthinkingly held him up to the contempt and ridicule of her family and his neighbors.

She would have to reach Tom first and explain to him how much her views had altered in the month she had been married. She hardly knew how to understand herself, and she would appear self-contradictory and foolish to her sensible brother. The husband she had been so sure she did not want was gone, and she felt his absence every hour.

"Well, lass," came a voice from the stable behind her.

Bel turned. "Good morning, Mr. Farre," she said. She looked across the gravel drive at Courtland. Its top windows were just catching the sun and blazing into fiery brilliance. She could not spend another day there thinking of Nick every minute.

Farre was standing beside her. "Did you want a horse saddled, lass?" he asked.

"No, thank you, Mr. Farre," Bel replied. "I think I . . . will walk into the village today."

Later, as she walked along Bel had every reason to congratulate herself on her plan. The dew on the grass, the song of a thrush, the pleasure of her own brisk stride restored her. She greeted a farmer leading his cow to market, gathered a bouquet of bright red poppies and purple harebells and sticky, fragrant strands of honeysuckle, and had quite forgotten to think of her husband for whole minutes at a time.

Then she saw Auggie approaching from the opposite end of the lane with Honey trotting at his heels.

Auggie had been avoiding her quite successfully for
days. He had his rod and basket, and Bel could guess
his destination. She hoped he would not notice her
until it was too late to avoid the encounter, but the
dog at his side could not be fooled. Honey barked
and came bounding ahead to greet Bel. Auggie
checked his stride an instant, then hurried to the
break in the hedge where the path to the Lower Ashe
began. He disappeared from sight.

"Auggie," Bel called.

There was no answer, but Honey, barking excitedly, darted through the hedge after Auggie. The
barking stopped, and the dog came bounding back
into the lane. She came up to Bel, wagging her tail
with such vigor that it seemed to shake her whole
body. She dropped at Bel's feet and rolled onto her
back, encouraging Bel to rub and pat her silky chest.
From beyond the hedge came a piercing whistle that
brought Honey to her feet once more. She trotted to
the hedge and barked in confusion.

Bel marched up to the opening.

"Auggie Shaw," she called, "your dog has better
manners than you do."

Then he appeared, stomping along, muttering.

"Stupid dog," he said to Honey, who began jump-
ing up and down around the two of them. "Down,"
Auggie commanded, and the dog dropped at his feet.

"What do you want, Bel?" he asked.

"To say hello," she said.

"Where are you going?"

"To town," she replied.

"Walking?" I thought you had a dozen fine carriages to ride in now."

"I like walking, Auggie. What are you doing?"

He shrugged and looked at the rod in his hands.
"Fishing."

"Alone?"

"I'm meeting a friend," he said. He looked at the dust of the lane and toed it with his boot.

"Do you know who your friends are, Auggie?" she asked, looking at the dejected slump of his shoulders.

"I know who they aren't." He shot her an angry glance.

Bel tried another tack. "What about Arthur and Phil—aren't they going with you?"

"All they do is study for smalls."

"You could, too," Bel suggested.

"Not me. I'm the only one that's not going anywhere. Tom and you, you left. Phil and Arthur will go, too. Not me. I'm the one that's going to stay and fish like we always did."

Bel took a deep breath and watched her brother closely. "Do you think you'll catch anything on the Lower? Dozens of fish were poisoned on the earl's stretch little more than a week ago."

He showed no surprise, but lifted his head, his eyes cold, his chin tilted up defiantly. "I know."

"Do you think Tom would respect what you're doing, Auggie?" she asked.

"Do you think Tom's going to respect you? At least I stick by my friends and don't go off after titles and riches."

"Darlington is not your friend," she said. "I don't know why he's doing what he's doing, but it's foolish and hurtful."

"He *is* my friend. He was Tom's friend and now he's mine. You are not on our side anymore, Bel. You stopped being on our side that day we went up to Courtland in the pony cart."

Bel felt a slight flush creep into her cheeks. "It's not a matter of sides, is it?" she asked. "The earl is part of our family now."

"He's no Shaw."

"But we have to let him be one of us."

"The fellow who took *our* stream? Hah!"

"It's not just our stream, Auggie, and at least he respects it. He's not poisoning trout."

"You defend him because you like his kisses. You kissed him that day we went up there. I know you did."

"Kisses don't make enemies."

"Don't they? You're my enemy, Bel." He gave her one last burning glare, then snapped his fingers at Honey and turned and stepped through the hedge again. The dog whimpered once and nuzzled Bel's hand. Bel responded with a quick ruffling of the golden head, then a command that sent the dog bounding after Auggie.

Bel stood in the lane where the whole troubling summer had begun. Tonight Tom would be home. Whose side would he be on?

Bel crossed her room for the third or fourth time. Daylight faded at her windows, and she gauged the hour yet again. She told herself she was perfectly ready for the evening. She was certainly satisfied with her appearance. Her new gown of pale blue figured muslin seemed like a piece of summer sky. It was gathered below her breasts with a length of creamy ribbon, and about her shoulders she wore a matching shawl with a blue border. All that remained of her preparations was to fix in her mind the precise phrases she must use to convince Tom of Nick's worthiness to be her husband.

Her first point was to be that Nick could not be faulted for purchasing and restoring an available property. Then she would explain how extremely forbearing he had been about the attacks against his stream and buildings. Next she would point out his generosity to the Shaws once he had connected himself to them. It would not hurt, she thought, to mention that Nick was a fine angler and loved the Ashe as much as any Shaw. As to his conduct toward herself, though she had at first accused him of arrogance and ungentlemanly behavior, he had in fact rescued her on more than one occasion and had treated her with the utmost respect and courtesy since their wedding. She faltered and her steps slowed a little.

Her brother was bound to ask the one question for which she had no answer. *"Does he love you?"* Tom would ask. Much as she would like to be sure that she could answer that question with ringing conviction, she knew she could not. It was the very question that had plagued her in recent days. Did Nick love her? If he did, when had he begun? Surely, if he did love her, she could point to some evidence of that love in his words or actions. But just when she believed his desire for her had increased, he had stopped asking for the bargain kisses.

A knock on the connecting door between their bedrooms startled her out of her thoughts. Slowly she crossed to the door.

"Bel?" came Nick's voice from his room.

She fumbled with the key and managed to open the door.

"You're home," she said. He was the shepherd. She took in his dusty boots and wind-ruffled hair and the patch of sunburn across his cheeks and the bridge of his nose.

"Yes, I'm . . . home." He said the word with a hesitant wonder. "Are you going out? Has your brother arrived?"

She nodded. Something had changed in him. His eyes were quite as black as they had ever been, but more alive than she had ever seen them. She was reminded of the first time she had seen him smile, of sunlight sparkling off the clear surface of the Ashe.

"May I join you? It will take me but a few minutes to change."

She thought of her speech for Tom. "Do you wish to come? Are you not tired from your journey?"

"I'm fine. It feels good to be . . . home. No clocks."

Undecided, she stared at him, and something of her feelings must have appeared on her face, for his smile faded a bit. She wanted him to come, but he must not meet Tom before she had an opportunity to explain herself to her brother. She twisted her hands together in the folds of her shawl, and lowered her gaze from his.

He stepped forward and reached out, taking her hands in his and rubbing his thumbs across the backs of her hands soothingly. "It's all right," he said. "It's a family thing, I know. I don't have to be there. I can meet your brother on another occasion."

She lifted her eyes to his and shook her head. "No," she said, "I want you to come. Come, please." She squeezed the hands that held hers.

He released her and stepped back and nodded. Then he grinned and began to strip off his jacket. With some confusion she excused herself and closed the door between them. She leaned against the door while her heart raced. She prayed she would reach Tom first.

At first glance Nick saw that Captain Tom Shaw had *hero* written all over him, from the gold epaulettes on his broad shoulders to the gleam of his polished boots. The blue eyes, alive with the quick intelligence of all the Shaws, had a heightened intensity in his bronzed face. Though the captain appeared perfectly at ease, there was nothing indolent in his stance. He stood as straight as the mast of his ship. Only the captain's eyes suggested the energy he held in check in his mother's drawing room. Only the captain's unruly fair hair suggested his kinship with young Master Augustus Shaw at his side.

At second glance Nick saw that the captain had an extraordinary effect on the Shaws. While they were not precisely quiet, they seemed to be listening to one another more than Nick had ever observed them to do before. It was as if Tom Shaw's own air of quiet, alert interest in the world around him had spread to the rest of his family. Even the dog sat still at the captain's feet, her ears up in an attitude of patient readiness.

The captain took in Nick's presence with the same easy energy with which he seemed to control the room. Tom Shaw's quick blue gaze lighted first on Bel, and for a moment a smile restored his features to a youthfulness that rivaled his sister's. But when that same blue gaze met Nick's, there was a perceptible hardening of the captain's expression, and Nick knew he was being sized up as an adversary. He did not even blink. At Haverly he had discovered a truth so powerful, so bright and piercing, he felt as if he had seized a magic sword. He loved Bel.

He loved her so much that he could give her up if she wished him to, or fight dragons to keep her if he must. He nodded at Tom Shaw. The evening would bring them together sooner or later.

Bel felt she had never been more distracted in her life. The excitement of seeing Tom safe and whole and yet altered by his years at sea, the necessity to speak to him alone, and the sense that Darlington and Auggie had already further prejudiced Tom's view of Nick kept her from any close attention to the remarks of those around her. More than once she had received odd looks at answers she believed to be perfectly unexceptional until she attempted to recall what her companion had been saying. And the evening wore on without the opportunity she was longing for.

At one point, in passing her, with Ellen clinging to his sleeve, Tom had leaned Bel's way and whispered, "I got your letters, all of them." And he seemed to invest this remark with such significance that Bel's knees gave way a little, and she was compelled to lean heavily on her escort's arm for a step.

It was hours before the moment that Nick had anticipated arrived. He had been introduced to the captain early on, but it was not until the tea tray was brought in after supper that the shifting of guests at the party allowed the two men a chance to talk. Bel was settled on a sofa at the far end of the room, engaged in conversation with Ellen and Mrs. Fletcher and Phil. She looked up, alarm evident in her eyes, as Nick turned to Tom, but Nick took the step anyway.

"Haverly," said the captain in his low crisp tones, "I think you should know that I received certain letters from my sister, written between May and July this year. The letters, which are still in my possession, raise serious doubts in my mind about your behavior toward my sister."

Nick raised an eyebrow. He could imagine the sorts of things she had said about him in May. "What do you doubt, Captain Shaw?" he asked.

"That you love my sister, that you mean to be the sort of husband she deserves."

"Those are serious doubts," Nick agreed mildly. He found it very satisfying to watch the tightening of the captain's jaw. Tom Shaw was not as cool as he first appeared.

"I want an explanation, Haverly," the captain demanded with as much force as their circumstances allowed.

"Fine," said Nick. "When and where?"

"Tomorrow, dawn."

Nick looked into the fierce blue eyes and taut, angry face of his opponent. "Dawn?" he asked, unable to resist a certain ironic inflection in saying it.

Tom Shaw looked as if he were tempted to laugh,

but he evidently controlled the impulse. "I don't mean pistols, Haverly."

"Good," said Nick. "I don't have any. Where?"

"You name the place."

Nick looked up briefly and saw that Auggie Shaw and Darlington were watching his exchange with Tom Shaw. If the captain was aware of them he didn't show it. Nick shrugged. For once in his life he had nothing to fear or to hide, and he would definitely relish fighting for Bel. In fact, he had been wanting to fight someone or something all summer. So he said to the captain, "The Thill cottage is empty. Do you know the place?"

The captain nodded.

"I will be there," Nick said. He turned and strolled across the drawing room toward his love.

Some confusion at the end of the evening required that Bel and Nick convey Uncle Fletcher home in their carriage, so Bel was obliged to wait for an opportunity to speak to her husband about the quiet exchange she had observed between him and her brother. Then on the stairs, just as she readied herself to begin her confession, her husband had excused himself and descended to his library.

Taken by surprise, Bel had continued up to her room. She found her maid waiting and gently dismissed the girl. For a few moments she considered that perhaps there was no need for alarm, that her brother and husband might not have touched on the matters contained in her letters. She untied her slippers and folded her shawl. She removed her necklace and ear-bobs and began to pull the pins from her hair. But such complacency was impossible to maintain. She knew her brother's willingness to defend her. She had seen the smug looks on the faces of Auggie and Darlington as Nick and Tom talked. And she knew her husband would meet any challenge.

With a flash of insight it occurred to her that her husband would wait until he believed her asleep before he returned to his room. Carefully she trimmed the lamps, leaving just a single candle burning where its glow could not be seen under the door or through the window, and she waited.

Her patience was soon rewarded by the quiet click of the door to her husband's room. With equal quietness she turned the key of the connecting door and pulled it open. He was crossing his bedroom, his boots in one hand, his jacket and cravat and waistcoat draped over his other arm, his white cambric shirt loose about him—her shephard. He froze at her opening the door, then turned to face her.

"I have something to ask you and something to tell you," she said.

"Where would you like to begin?" he asked, putting his boots down and dropping his clothes on a chair. He took a few steps in her direction but when his gaze took in her bare feet and loose hair, he stopped.

She drew herself up. "Have you agreed to meet my brother?"

"Not for a duel, if that's what you're fearing."

"But you have agreed to meet him?"

"He'd like an explanation of how you came to be married to me so abruptly, and it seems fair enough to give him one."

"I think that my brother already harbors an unjust opinion of how we came to be married." She took a deep breath. "You see, I . . . wrote to him about . . . our first meeting and your accusations and . . . I even mentioned that we had made a bargain and that you would be demanding your 'pound of flesh.' "

"Your brother mentioned your letters," Nick said quietly.

"So you see, I ought to meet him to explain, not you," she pleaded.

"I don't see," he said bluntly. "Your brother has every right to hold me accountable for my behavior toward you." He paused. "I think he will find the truth acceptable."

"The truth?"

Nick lowered his eyes from hers. She was entirely too tempting to look at with her hair down and her toes peeking from beneath the hem of her gown. "I think your brother should know that an annulment is still possible, with a generous settlement for you, of course," he finished, as coolly as he could.

Bel reached for the door frame and held tightly. That was their agreement, but he made it sound less a matter of her choice than a foregone conclusion. Sometime while he had been away at Haverly, he had apparently given up on their marriage. Well, she could hardly blame him for that. He had allied himself with a family too proud to see the merit and worth of one outside their own fair circle, with a wife so proud she must wait to see her husband humble himself before she would admit to a desire to enter his bed.

She tried a smile. "So when do you meet my brother?"

Nick looked up. Her false brightness did not deceive him. "Tomorrow . . . afternoon," he lied. "It will be quite civilized. There will be others around." He hoped that would throw her off a bit.

"Oh," she said. "So I ought to bid you good night?"

"Yes," he said.

There was something in that strained syllable that reminded her of other moments between them, moments when she had been sure he desired her. She straightened and released her hold on the door frame. "Do you want a bargain kiss?" she asked.

"Lord," he said with sudden vehemence, "I blackmailed you into that bargain, and it's cost you much more than the kisses we agreed to that day. No, I do not want a *bargain* kiss. I release you from that bargain."

Bel thought she had never seen him truly angry before; his eyes were snapping, his fists closing and unclosing at his sides. Her ploy had failed, and it did not seem to be the moment to offer to come to his bed as she might have found the courage to do if he had been holding her and kissing her. She called on her reserves of pride.

"Thank you," she said. "Good night then."

"Good night," he said.

She turned and firmly closed the door. He did not love her.

Nick stared blankly at the closed door. He had not meant to release her in quite that way, but the temptation to seize her and drag her to his bed had been growing upon him from the moment she'd opened the door between their rooms.

He turned and sank into the chair that held his clothes. Lord, he could fight anyone right now—twice.

19

eeeeeeeeeee

$\mathbf{T}$HE SUN'S BRIGHT rim was just visible above the wooded hills to the east when Nick reined in at Thill cottage. Somewhere nearby a horse whinnied, and from the cottage itself he could hear voices. He dismounted, pulled the reins over his mount's head, and secured them to a sturdy branch of the hedge surrounding the cottage yard. He stretched his arms above his head, then shook them, loosening the tension in his body. Then he stepped up to the opening in the hedge.

Before him was a patch of unscythed grass, yellow from late summer heat, and beyond it at the cottage door stood Tom and Auggie Shaw and Darlington. The captain was out of uniform, and Nick sensed that without the blue and gold reminders of his rank, Tom Shaw was apt to be much less restrained in his behavior than he had been the night before.

"Good morning, Haverly," said the captain. He turned and said a curt word to his companions and strode out into the yard to meet Nick.

Nick took a position with the hedge at his back and a clear view of the whole yard. Perhaps he should have brought Farre. "Good morning, Shaw," he said.

They stood face-to-face, not three yards apart.

"Haverly," the captain began, "my father is a fair

man, and I try to be a fair man, so I will tell you what I've heard and listen to what you have to say."

Nick nodded.

"My sister's letters call you arrogant. Her friends tell me you have insulted her and all the Shaws more than once, accused her and my brothers of crimes and threatened them with legal action. And you used some bargain to gain power over my sister. Your title and wealth may have weighed with my parents but never with Bel. Can you explain to me, then, why my sweet sister chose to separate herself from her family and friends by wedding a man she clearly disliked a month ago?"

"Your sister married me to preserve her honor and protect her family," said Nick, choosing his words carefully and watching the restless shifting of the captain's body. Darlington and Auggie had stepped up behind Tom Shaw on either side of him.

"To preserve her honor?" Tom asked.

"I compromised her," Nick admitted.

"You arrogant bastard," shouted Tom, lunging forward with his left foot and bringing his right fist around in an arching upward drive. Nick's own right fist shot out in a cross-stroke, blocking the intended blow with his forearm. He felt the shock of it from his teeth to his toes. Then he felt Darlington grab him from behind, pinning his arms. He quelled the impulse to struggle and looked squarely at Tom Shaw.

Even knowing that her husband had lied to her about his appointment with her brother, Bel was not prepared for the perfidy of his sneaking out of the house at dawn. The quiet closing of his door disturbed her sleep, but she did not quite comprehend the sound until a few minutes later when she heard the hooves of his horse on the gravel of the drive. It would be a dawn meeting, of course. She threw off the covers·and hurried through hasty ablutions and a most careless donning of habit, half-boots, and shawl.

When she burst into the stable, she was surprised to discover Farre saddling a horse.

"Oh, Mr. Farre, how did you know I would wish to go after him?" she asked.

Farre stopped and fixed her with a look she could hardly consider approving.

"Didn't," he said. "I was fixing to go after him myself, you see, but I never had it in my mind for you to go. No, his *lordship* wouldn't like that."

"But, Mr. Farre, my brother thinks ill of him most unjustly and will do him serious harm, and it's all my fault."

"Now lass, I promise you, your brother is going to be thinking just as he ought to about the lad in no time and with no help from you."

"Mr. Farre, I cannot have my brother think ill of my husband. I must prevent this meeting."

"Cannot have your brother disliking your husband? And why is that, lass? Become fond of the lad, have you?"

Farre's gaze was penetrating, and there was no use denying her feelings to him. He had probably recognized her love for Nick before she had. He had seen her mooning about in Nick's absence.

"I have," she said.

"Well then, let me saddle another horse. I have a fair idea of where they're like to meet, and I'll bring you along. But one word, and I'll drag you off, mistress or no."

"Mr. Farre," she asked as he turned to his task, "why are you going after him?"

Farre grinned. "Lass, 'twas I who taught the lad to mill."

When they neared the deserted cottage which Farre suspected as the meeting place, he insisted they tether the horses in a copse and make their way on foot. He led them in a wide circle around the cottage and brought them up to a place where a break in the hedge permitted a view of the cottage yard. The sight that greeted them caused Bel to suck in her breath. Darlington held Nick fast, and it appeared that Tom meant to pound his fists into her helpless husband. Farre raised a finger to his lips, silencing her. She strained to catch the words of the men in the yard over the pounding of her heart.

"Let him go, Darlington," Tom offered. "This will be a fair fight." He turned and began to strip off his jacket.

Darlington lifted his right knee and shoved hard against Nick's back, releasing Nick's arms only at the last moment so that Nick went sprawling in the grass.

"Hey," yelled Auggie, drawing Bel's gaze to him. He stared at Darlington as if he'd never seen him before.

Darlington winked at the boy. "All's fair in love and war," he said.

Bel turned her gaze back to Nick, who pushed himself up, stood, and tore off his jacket. He opened the neck of his shirt, loosened the cuffs, pulled the garment up over his head, and tossed it aside on the grass.

As he did it, Bel felt the familiar quiver start in her. She had seen his strength in the things he did, had felt it when his arms were around her, but she had never guessed that it meant this swell and play of muscle or breadth of shoulder.

Tom advanced toward Nick, and the two of them began to circle warily, face-to-face, fists raised. It was her chance to act. She could shout and rush into the yard. She could proclaim her love for Nick, and whatever Nick felt for her, Tom would respect her choice. Farre shot Bel a warning glance, and she understood him. Tom would respect Nick for standing up to him. She could not take that away from her husband. She raised her own clenched fists to her mouth, biting down on the knuckle of her right fore-finger to keep from making a sound.

"Draw his cork, Tom" Auggie shouted.

"Take him down, Shaw," Darlington added.

Nick feinted, and Tom made a wide swing that cut the air.

"I may have compromised your sister, but I did marry her. Her reputation is safe," Nick told his ad-versary.

"What kind of man compromises young women of gentle birth?" taunted Darlington.

"Not women," said Nick, never taking his eyes off Tom, "just Bel."

Tom made a move then that deceived Nick into protecting his face and taking a series of blows to his ribs and belly, before he countered with a strong right to Tom's shoulder.

"Ask him how he got her alone in my mother's garden," Darlington advised Tom.

"Well, Haverly?" Tom said.

"We had a . . . bargain," Nick said. The word drew another heavy blow from Tom.

"You blackmailed her, Haverly," shouted Darling-ton.

"I did," Nick admitted.

"With what threat?" asked Tom. "My sister's the soul of principle and discretion. What could you hold against her? What could you gain from her?"

"That's between me and your sister," Nick an-swered.

"What kind of answer is that?" demanded Tom. He jabbed lightly at Nick's jaw with his right, draw-ing an answering punch from Nick, then slamming into Nick's ribs with his left. Nick spun away from the blow, striking out with an unorthodox backhanded right that caught Tom squarely in the upper chest.

Both men stepped back, breathing hard, their bodies gleaming with the sweat of their exertions.

"Ask him what their bargain was," urged Darlington.

Tom shot a quizzical glance at his friend and then looked back at Nick.

"We had a bargain," Nick repeated doggedly. "It was just between us. And your sister is free of it now."

Tom Shaw stepped back a bit further. "What do you mean she's free now?" He paused for breath. "She's shackled for life to a man who doesn't love her."

"I didn't say ... I didn't love her, Shaw," Nick said.

Behind the hedge Bel caught her breath and drew a stern look from Farre.

Tom lowered his fists. "Wait a minute," he said. "Did you compromise my sister or not, Haverly?"

"He kissed her," said Auggie with a doubtful air. Tom spun to look at his brother with a glare that would have quelled the cockiest junior officer on his ship. Auggie refused to meet Tom's eye. "The whole county knew," he added.

"Kissed her?" said Tom in disgust. "Auggie, you and Darlington have been implying he raped her. How did the whole county know? Did he brag about the stolen kisses in the taproom?"

Auggie shook his head.

Tom turned to Darlington.

"Who are you going to believe, Tom," Darlington asked, "your friends or some high-in-the-instep stranger who comes to Ashecombe and lords it over the rest of us?"

"I'd like to believe the man who tells me the truth."

"And you think I'm lying to you, Tom? I'm the one that found them in my mother's garden."

"Are you the one that told the world what they were doing there?" Tom asked a bit sadly.

"You're going to blame me?" Darlington cried. "This fellow traps your sister into some bargain that she calls a 'pound of flesh'—that's what you told me, isn't it—and insults your brothers, and you attack me?"

Tom turned wearily to Nick. "This is not much of a mill, Haverly, but it still could be if I can figure out who I've really got to fight. And it all comes down to this: what was the damn bargain you made with my sister?"

Nick smiled. Bel saw in her husband that joyful transforming look she had first seen in him when he returned from Haverly. And she clenched her fists tighter to keep from crying out in answer to it.

"It was a *sweet* bargain, Shaw," Nick said, "and I promised—"

"But I know," interrupted Auggie, turning to Tom. "I know when you made it. The day we came in the pony cart, and I saw . . . well, that's when she started to change. I know what it was—"

"Auggie!" Nick's voice rang out sharp and clear.

Auggie spun to face Nick.

"Don't tell," Nick said. "I promised your sister."

Auggie stared at Nick as if he had forgotten the other two men, and to Bel it seemed that in her younger brother's eyes was a new understanding. Auggie, too, had seen the look on Nick's face and read it. At last the boy nodded. "But I'm going to tell something else," he said. He tilted up the defiant Shaw chin. "Arthur and I put the bread on the pool. Darlington bought it for us in Hilcombe. And we did some . . . other things, too."

"You set fire to the timbers?" Nick asked.

Auggie shook his head. He pointed at Darlington.

"Did you poison the fish?"

"With Darlington," Auggie confessed.

"Then I owe your sister an apology for blaming you and your brother for the worst of the damage."

"Does that mean I'll get my cap back?" Auggie asked. "I saw it through the window on your desk."

"Will you leave my—*the* river as you find it?"

Auggie nodded.

"Then you can have your cap back." Nick grinned.

With a sudden bound Auggie crossed the circle to stand by Nick and face the other two.

"Well, I like that backhanded turn, Auggie Shaw," said Darlington, his lip curling. "You're just like your sister. You're just like all the Shaws—proud as sin, until there's someone grander and richer than yourselves. Then we see how mercenary you all are. You sell yourself for a stream. She sells herself to the highest bidder."

"Darlington, enough," snapped Tom. "What's come over you, man?" He turned toward his friend.

Darlington stood with his feet planted, his fists clenched, his body leaning aggressively forward. "Your sister made a mockery of me. Everyone knew she was mine, but she was too proud for a squire's kisses. Then she falls into this fellow's arms like a lightskirt. You should have seen them, Shaw, you—"

Tom Shaw's fist shot out again, this time directed toward his friend's nose, but Nick leapt between the two men, batting aside Tom's arm and catching a blow in the back from Darlington.

"This is my fight," Nick said to the astonished Tom. "She's my wife. I have the right to defend her honor."

Tom raised his hands and backed away.

Nick turned to Darlington, facing him across a few feet of dry summer grass.

"She was supposed to be mine, not yours, Haverly," declared Darlington, pulling off his coat. His waistcoat and shirt soon followed, and the two men began the wary circling of each other that Bel had first seen Tom and Nick do. But where Tom and Nick were evenly matched in size, Darlington was taller than Nick by three or four inches and clearly outweighed him by a stone or more.

In spite of his opponent's greater size, Nick was grinning, and Bel sensed a relish in him for this fight that he had not shown in sparring with her brother.

"You can't fool me, Haverly," said Darlington. "You haven't had her yet." Darlington's right fist shot out, headed for Nick's face, but with a slight tipping of his head, Nick avoided the blow while his own left slammed into Darlington's midsection, lifting the bigger man briefly onto his toes.

"Darlington, for the last time, I will not allow you to talk about Bel as a piece of property to be possessed," Nick said through clenched teeth.

Bel kept her fist pressed tightly to her mouth. It was terrible and wonderful, her husband's willingness to trade these thudding blows for her. She flinched at the impact of fist and flesh, but in the driving blows her husband released an intensity he had held in check all summer. She stole a glance at Farre, who raised an eyebrow in answer to her look. She smiled. Her shephard was hardly a porcelain figure.

Again and again Darlington's big fists drove at Nick, but most of the intended blows missed. With that easy movement Bel had seen in Nick when he climbed their tree, he leaned or ducked or spun, and when he wanted to land a blow himself, he let Darlington charge into it so that the man's own weight worked against him. Darlington was working much harder at the fight than his opponent, but Bel sensed her husband was waiting for something.

Then it came. Darlington lunged tiredly, putting his weight into a driving right that passed just over

Nick's shoulder as Nick's own right fist came up and collided with Darlington's nose with a resounding crack.

"You've drawn his cork," Auggie shouted, leaping into the air.

Darlington fell back, swearing and clutching his wounded face. Tom stepped up and clapped Nick on the back.

Farre tugged at Bel's sleeve, gave her a smug look, and with a tip of his head urged her away from their vantage point. Reluctantly, Bel drew her eyes from the vision of her triumphant husband shaking her brother's hand. As much as she wanted Nick to confirm for her ears alone the love he had just confessed, she wanted him to enjoy her brothers' friendship.

In the copse Bel discovered that her horse, hastily tethered, had gotten loose and wandered off. She thought briefly of appealing to Farre for his mount, but one look at the man's face told her that he thought even a countess must pay for her own carelessness. She would have to curb her impatience to return to Courtland.

Nick settled himself in the bath with hardly any lessening of the pleasure he'd been feeling from the moment his fists had first connected with Darlington's very substantial person. Though his muscles ached, and a colorful assortment of bruises had begun to flower on his ribs and back, he had ended Darlington's claims to Bel. And he had parted from Bel's brothers on such terms of amity that he thought they would always remain his friends even if Bel should choose the annulment he could now offer her.

He soaked his head and washed the dust and sweat and blood from his face. Then he leaned back against the high copper lip of the bath and closed his eyes and let himself imagine that Bel would refuse the annulment and declare her love for him. This thought led to so many pleasant images that he lost all sense of time and was startled by a knock on the door of his dressing room. He pulled himself up in the tepid water and glanced about for his towel. Farre would have gotten word at the stable of Nick's victory.

"Come in," he called.

The door opened slowly, setting the steam that had drifted up from the bath into swirling eddies. Then Bel stepped into the room. Her face was flushed, tendrils of golden hair had escaped their pins, her eyes were wide with surprise and, Nick knew, awareness of him. He was having difficulty breathing himself.

Bel stared at her husband. A cut marred the fine edge of one brow, his lower lip was swollen, and she could see the irregular shape of a purplish bruise on his left shoulder. She wanted very much to touch each spot, but at the same time, her legs trembled under her, and she did not dare move.

"I know what happened," she said. "I saw you fight them."

"How?" he asked.

"Farre led me there. We watched from behind the hedge," she admitted.

"We should talk," he said.

She nodded.

"I can't talk rationally to you . . . like this," he confessed.

"Of course not," she said. "I'll go and let you . . ."

"No." His voice was a little thicker than he wished it to be. He swallowed and tried again. "Just turn." He made a little circling gesture with the fingers of one hand, and she turned her back to him.

He took a deep breath and gripped the sides of the bath. With sudden resolution he levered his aroused body from the water and stood. He grabbed his towel, hastily applied it to his head and shoulders, wrapped it securely about him, and turned to his wife.

Bel stood with her back to her husband, scarcely able to breathe. She tried to contain the trembling feeling inside by crossing her arms and gripping tight to her elbows. The moment that she had been unwilling to face on her wedding day had come. It was terrible to leave the circle of love and trust in which she had been Bel Shaw all her life, but it would be wonderful now, she knew, to enter the circle of this man's arms.

Then her husband's arms came around her and his lips brushed her cheek.

"I—" he started to say.

She turned in his arms and pressed her fingers to his lips, shaking her head.

"Me first," she said, gazing frankly into his eyes. But what she saw there was too much even for her new understanding of desire. She lowered her eyes, and for a few minutes lost herself in contemplation of the hollows at the base of his throat and the pulse beating strongly under her hands. Then she found her voice again. "Much as I love my family, much as I will always care for them," she vowed solemnly, "they cannot come between us. You are first with me." She lifted her eyes to his. "I love you."

Nick could not speak, so he tightened his hold on her, lowered his lips to hers, let himself be lost in kisses he did not have to count, quick touches of his mouth to all the features that were dear to him, sensuous brushes of his lips against hers, long slow yieldings of his spirit to her spirit, until he had to pull back one last time.

"I was going to offer you an annulment," he told her.

She shook her head.

He swallowed. "There are two things . . . I must tell you," he said. He paused to steady his breathing.

"I love you. I have dreamed of making love to you from the first day when you stood in the Ashe in the sunlight." His words provoked a very fervent response from his wife, and it was some time before he could again marshal his thoughts.

"Second," he said.

She laughed.

"I . . . can't do the things I've been dreaming of now because . . . I have invited your entire family to dinner here."

Bel drew back in his arms and looked at him incredulously. He was grinning at her, and she thought happiness made his already handsome face quite beautiful. "You invited all of them here?" She could hardly comprehend this change in him.

He nodded, bringing up a hand to stroke her cheek and distracting her for several seconds. "When are they to come?" she asked.

"Four," he said. "What time is it?"

"It's twenty minutes later than you think it is," she said.

"So it is." He laughed. He took her by the shoulders, turned her around, and marched her to the dressing-room door. She looked at him over her shoulder with such reluctance to leave plain in her eyes that he nearly lost his resolve. But he had not fought his own desires so long, waiting for the something more that had eluded him, that he could not wait a few more hours for love.

"Go," he said firmly. "You don't want Aunt Margaret to find the food wanting at Courtland."

Epilogue

BEL LAY IN the warmth of her husband's arms, marveling at the completeness of their union. A line of poetry she had considered mere pretty words came back to her. *The soul transpires at every pore with instant fires.* It had been like that. Her skin which had been indifferent to the touch of silks had awakened to his touch and could not yet endure the separation that sleep must bring. She pressed more closely against him, and he stirred.

"Are you asleep?" she asked.

"No," came the reply. "Do you want to talk?"

"Yes."

"Would you mind if I lit a lamp?" he asked.

She hesitated. It was wonderful and terrible to lie in his naked embrace in the dark. It made her tremble, but she had allowed him every touch in the shadowy darkness. Now she was uncertain of the light. Still she consented. He pulled his arms from around her, rolled away, and stretched across the bed to the table that held a lamp.

While he fumbled with the lamp, she pushed herself up against the pillows, and as she did so the covers fell away, exposing her shoulders and breasts. She grabbed the sheet, intending to restore her modesty, when an indrawn breath from her husband stopped her.

He had turned back to her and was staring reverently at her body. She tugged at the sheet, and he looked up.

"I'm sorry," he said. "I am rather susceptible to your charms."

"I'll put something on," she offered.

"No." He smiled. "I like you ... in white." He drew the sheet up then, tucking it around her, outlining her shape, his hands lingering here and there.

Then he fell back against the pillows beside her, an arm flung up over his eyes.

"You said you thought me a pastoral figure. Now you know. If I am a pastoral figure, it's a satyr."

"No," she said, "you are the passionate shepherd. 'Come live with me and be my love, and we will all the pleasures prove.'"

"You know I like ... proving pleasures," he said, moving his arm and looking at her with considerable desire in his dark eyes. "But I wonder if you will want to be desired quite as much as I desire you."

"I do," she assured him. "You will never have to count kisses again."

"You won't think me arrogant if I presume to take them from you?"

"You are not arrogant. Indeed, you have to cultivate more *pride*, not less, if you wish to be allied with a Shaw."

"More pride?" he exclaimed, pushing himself up and leaning on one side toward her. "The last thing your family needs is to accept a person with more pride."

"Are you insulting my family, sir?" she demanded.

"Never," he said. "But I warn you, I mean to set up a rival family, right here on the banks of the Ashe.

She looked at him.

"The Seymours. I want a dozen dark-eyed, dark-haired sons and daughters."

"A dozen?"

"At least a half dozen," he replied. He was looking at her with a marked intensity. "Do you want the light out?"

"Yes." She smiled. "For now."

Avon Regency Romance

Kasey Michaels

THE CHAOTIC MISS CRISPINO
76300-1/$3.99 US/$4.99 Can

THE DUBIOUS MISS DALRYMPLE
89908-6/$2.95 US/$3.50 Can

THE HAUNTED MISS HAMPSHIRE
76301-X/$3.99 US/$4.99 Can

THE WAGERED MISS WINSLOW
76302-8/$3.99 US/$4.99 Can

Loretta Chase

THE ENGLISH WITCH 70660-1/$2.95 US/$3.50 Can
ISABELLA 70597-4/$2.95 US/$3.95 Can
KNAVES' WAGER 71363-2/$3.95 US/$4.95 Can
THE SANDALWOOD PRINCESS
71455-8/$3.99 US/$4.99 Can

THE VISCOUNT VAGABOND
70836-1/$2.95 US/$3.50 Can

Jo Beverley

EMILY AND THE DARK ANGEL
71555-4/$3.99 US/$4.99 Can

THE STANFORTH SECRETS
71438-8/$3.99 US/$4.99 Can

Avon Romances—
the best in exceptional authors and unforgettable novels!

LORD OF MY HEART Jo Beverley
76784-8/$4.50 US/$5.50 Can

BLUE MOON BAYOU Katherine Compton
76412-1/$4.50 US/$5.50 Can

SILVER FLAME Hannah Howell
76504-7/$4.50 US/$5.50 Can

TAMING KATE Eugenia Riley
76475-X/$4.50 US/$5.50 Can

THE LION'S DAUGHTER Loretta Chase
76647-7/$4.50 US/$5.50 Can

CAPTAIN OF MY HEART Danelle Harmon
76676-0/$4.50 US/$5.50 Can

BELOVED INTRUDER Joan Van Nuys
76476-8/$4.50 US/$5.50 Can

SURRENDER TO THE FURY Cara Miles
76452-0/$4.50 US/$5.50 Can

Coming Soon

SCARLET KISSES Patricia Camden
76825-9/$4.50 US/$5.50 Can

WILDSTAR Nicole Jordan
76622-1/$4.50 US/$5.50 Can

Avon Romantic Treasures

*Unforgettable, enthralling love stories,
sparkling with passion and adventure
from Romance's bestselling authors*

ONLY IN YOUR ARMS *by Lisa Kleypas*
76150-5/$4.50 US/$5.50 Can

LADY LEGEND *by Deborah Camp*
76735-X/$4.50 US/$5.50 Can

RAINBOWS AND RAPTURE *by Rebecca Paisley*
76565-9/$4.50 US/$5.50 Can

AWAKEN MY FIRE *by Jennifer Horsman*
76701-5/$4.50 US/$5.50 Can

ONLY BY YOUR TOUCH *by Stella Cameron*
76606-X/$4.50 US/$5.50 Can

FIRE AT MIDNIGHT *by Barbara Dawson Smith*
76275-7/$4.50 US/$5.50 Can

ONLY WITH YOUR LOVE *by Lisa Kleypas*
76151-3/$4.50 US/$5.50 Can

MY WILD ROSE *by Deborah Camp*
76738-4/$4.50 US/$5.50 Can

America Loves Lindsey!

The Timeless Romances
of #1 Bestselling Author
Johanna Lindsey

ANGEL 75628-5/$5.99 US/$6.99 Can
He is called Angel—a ruggedly handsome hired gun with eyes as black as sin.

PRISONER OF MY DESIRE 75627-7/$5.99 US/$6.99 Can
Spirited Rowena Belleme *must* produce an heir, and the magnificent Warrick deChaville is the perfect choice to sire her child—though it means imprisoning the handsome knight.

ONCE A PRINCESS 75625-0/$5.95 US/$6.95 Can
From a far off land, a bold and brazen prince came to America to claim his promised bride. But the spirited vixen spurned his affections while inflaming his royal blood with passion's fire.

WARRIOR'S WOMAN 75301-4/$4.95 US/$5.95 Can

MAN OF MY DREAMS 75626-9/$5.99 US/$6.99 Can

Coming Soon
THE MAGIC OF YOU